HOLLOWTHORN

ALSO BY
KALYN JOSEPHSON

A RAVENFALL NOVEL

HOLLOWTHORN

KALYN JOSEPHSON

DELACORTE PRESS

Text copyright © 2023 by Kalyn Josephson
Jacket art copyright © 2023 by Ramona Kaulitzki

All rights reserved. Published in the United States by Delacorte Press, an imprint of Random House Children's Books, a division of Penguin Random House LLC, New York.

Delacorte Press is a registered trademark and the colophon is a trademark of Penguin Random House LLC.

Visit us on the Web! rhcbooks.com

Educators and librarians, for a variety of teaching tools, visit us at RHTeachersLibrarians.com

Library of Congress Cataloging-in-Publication Data is available upon request.
ISBN 978-0-593-48362-6 (trade) — ISBN 978-0-593-48364-0 (ebook)

The text of this book is set in 11-point Requiem Text.
Interior design by Ken Crossland

Printed in the United States of America
10 9 8 7 6 5 4 3 2 1
First Edition

For Joss and Shannon, and the magic of coffee shops

Last time, in *Ravenfall* . . .

With a single touch, thirteen-year-old Annabella Ballinkay can see death, a power she doesn't think is very useful compared to those of the rest of her psychic family. Asking people, *Hey, remember the time that person died?* isn't the best party trick. So while her family use their abilities to entertain guests and run Ravenfall Inn, their magical B&B in the town of Wick, Oregon, Anna does her best Cinderella impression and handles all the chores.

When fourteen-year-old Colin Pierce arrives after being separated from his older brother, Liam, Anna has a vision of his parents' recent deaths at the hands of a mysterious supernatural being, and she jumps at the chance to prove herself. Along with her mischievous cat, Max (who's actually a Jabberwocky, a dragon-like creature that helps spirits move on), Anna and Colin begin searching for the culprit.

Then Colin's world is flipped upside down when he learns that he and his family are all Ravens, guardians of the Shield between the human world and the Otherworld. To teach him how to use his powers, Anna's aunt Elaine (who reads auras) and her uncle Roy (a pyrokinetic) put Colin through Raven boot camp. Feeling like a superhero with his enhanced senses, speed, and strength, and with the ability to summon magical items from his parents' journal (which contains generations' worth of information on the supernatural), Colin can't wait to face down the killer.

Until he finds out who it is.

After Colin has a vision of an ancient warrior, the kids research the warrior's sigil with the help of Anna's sisters, Rose (an empath) and Kara (a telepath). Together, they discover that wraiths are permanently possessing the living, and that the Irish *King of the actual freaking Dead,* Fin Varra, is behind the deaths not only of Colin's parents but of several other Ravens.

With each Raven death, the Shield weakens. Soon Fin will be able to destroy it completely, allowing the spirits on the other side to emerge—and only Colin can stop him. Assisted by the Ballinkays, Colin plans to defeat Fin at the upcoming party for Samhain (the Celtic origin of Halloween), when the house lets down its wards and all manner of magical beings attend. The problems? It's a masquerade ball, *and* they have no idea what Fin looks like.

To locate Fin the night of the party, Anna uses her abilities to test people in the crowd until she finds someone who gives her a vision of Colin's parents' deaths. Colin and Fin face off, and Fin reveals that Colin is not only descended from him but has inherited some of his power. With his ancient body decaying, Fin intends to possess Colin and break what remains of the Shield.

While the Ballinkays desperately fight to keep the Shield intact, Colin battles Fin. Max sacrifices himself to give Colin more power, but even that isn't enough. As the Shield wanes and Colin begins to weaken, his older brother, Liam, emerges, having followed Fin to the Otherworld and gotten trapped. Together, he and Colin defeat Fin, saving the Shield.

Using the life magic he inherited from Fin, Colin resurrects Max, and everyone helps restore Ravenfall after the fight. Colin begins to process his difficult emotions and decides to stay at Ravenfall while Liam goes hunting, and Anna starts training with her clairvoyant mother, Nora, to learn about her own powers, which she now realizes are as important as anyone else's to Ravenfall.

CHAPTER I

Anna

E verything has a story.

 Some things are just more forthcoming than others. Take the worn silver coin Mr. Andrade brought me to read that morning—it wouldn't pipe down about jingling around in pockets or how it had spent a week wedged under the Andrades' kitchen table to even out a leg. I'd been able to tell Mr. Andrade four separate stories about the psychic uncle who'd owned it. Four!

My latest object hasn't made a peep.

Made of smooth, polished oak with a gold clasp, the chest is about the size of a small shoebox. There's an engraving of a patterned hand with the center three fingers straight up in a scout's salute, the thumb and pinky curving outward like petals at the base. In the middle of the palm is a wide, knowing eye that Colin said gave him the creeps. Something about it following him as he moved.

I found it in my dad's study among his cluttered collection of magical objects and have been trying and failing to read it for nearly half an hour.

"Relax, Anna," Nora says from beside me. My mother and I are sitting at the kitchen table, a plate of gingerbread cookies and a freshly poured cup of Earl Grey before each of us, courtesy of the house. I'd asked for Irish Breakfast, but there's no arguing when a four-story ancient inn puts its foot down.

"This sort of magic needs to flow naturally," Nora continues as she twists her blond curls up into a bun. "If you try to force it, you'll only stop it up."

Easy for her to say. She's been using her psychic powers for decades now; I've had my psychometry abilities for less than a year. But I try to do as she says and relax, to let my magic flow naturally to the chest. Nora told me to picture it like a bridge between me and the object, and then to cross that bridge to find information.

But my magic only sloughs off the engraved chest like melted snow.

I relinquish my white-knuckled grip on it and slump into my seat with a groan. "People are so much easier to read. Objects are the worst."

"People give their stories much more freely," Nora says reassuringly. "You'll get the hang of it eventually, like you did everything else."

I want to believe her, but I feel like I've come to a standstill. I made so much progress after Samhain thanks to Nora's lessons.

Before, if I touched someone who'd seen death, I got a vision of it too. Now I can control whether I get a vision when I touch someone, and I've begun to see other memories besides just people's deaths. But it's nearly mid-December now, and the only objects I've been able to read have been things like Mr. Andrade's coin, which'll shout at just about anybody with a magical pulse.

"I wanted to show Henry," I mutter, wrapping my hands around my mug and wishing my disappointment would evaporate with the steam. As a relic hunter, my dad would love to know the chest's history from its point of view. Soon I'll be able to tell him new things about everything he's collected, and maybe then he'll reconsider taking me on an expedition with him.

"Your father will be home all month." Nora scoots back her chair and stands. "You have plenty of time to figure it out. Speaking of which, I need to finish packing before Gran gets here."

"Do you even know what a suitcase looks like?" I tease. I'm thirteen, and I can't remember a single time Nora went on vacation. Uncle Roy and Aunt Elaine practically had to pry responsibility for the inn out of Nora's fingers to get her to go to Ireland with Gran for the week. She's spent the last few days writing little reminders and sticking them all over the house, as if we'd forget to make breakfast for the guests or redo the faerie wards on the garden just because she's not here.

"Ha, ha," Nora deadpans. "You know, it's not too late for me to cancel. Elaine can go and I can—"

"No!" I say it a little too quickly, and heat rushes to my cheeks.

It's not that I don't want Nora here; it's just that I've been looking forward to spending the week with my dad and hearing all about his latest adventure. If Nora's here, he'll just squirrel away in his study while she handles the inn since whenever he tries to help, he usually just ends up creating more work. Like the time he gave a guest directions to the magical hat shop downtown instead of the grocery store.

Besides, Nora deserves a break.

Nora gives me a knowing look, but mercifully lets it go. "I'll be upstairs. Can you take the challah out of the oven when the timer goes off?"

"Can't the house do it?"

She leans toward me and lowers her voice conspiratorially. "It's been dropping things lately. Don't tell it I told you—it's been grouchy about it."

The nearest wall groans, as if the house is leaning closer to hear. "But—" I start.

Nora presses a finger to her lips, glancing at the wall, before slipping out of the kitchen with a wink.

I stare mournfully at the chest.

My dad's been on one of his magical object expeditions for almost three months now, but he's finally coming home today, and I've been preparing all day in hopes of sharing the box's history with him as a welcome home present. I'm even wearing the Shalom Gnome sweater he got me right before he left in celebration of his return, the gnome's eyes hidden in a fluff of white beard and a low-slung beanie decorated in little Stars of David.

The house has felt empty without him, the trip one of the longest periods of time he's been gone, and I've been dying to tell him about everything that happened during Samhain. Colin's arrival after his parents' passing; his discovery that he's a Raven—one of the keepers of the Shield between our world and the Otherworld; our face-off against Fin Varra, the Irish King of the Dead, who was hunting down Ravens to weaken the Shield.

Henry always brings a story home with him from his adventures, but this time, I have one for him—and it's *epic*.

I pull Colin's Ravenguard journal over from the other side of the table and flip it open to the drawing of his Saint Knives that I've been working on. Thin black blades with veins of gold, they're a rare Raven weapon capable of killing powerful magical creatures. Even now, I can feel a bit of their power slipping through the pages, as if I could reach in and grab them just like Colin can.

The knives are the last thing left in his parents' journal that we need to transfer to this new one, and I've been working on the sketch for days, wanting to get them just right. Once we transfer the knives' magical connection to this new journal, Colin can bond with it and give the old one back to his brother, and then they'll both have their own Raven journal to summon things from.

I'm just shading in the last of the handles when the scent of char fills the air. Smoke begins to spill into the kitchen and I leap to my feet, trying to find a set of oven mitts. The side door flies open and Uncle Roy barrels in.

"Watch out!" he calls, and I step aside as he wrenches open the oven and drags the tray out bare-handed. He slides the blackened loaf of challah into the island sink, dousing it in water, and fans the smoke away with the tray.

"I sensed the smoke," he says to my bewildered look. I knew his pyrokinesis lets him summon and control flames, even making him impervious to heat, but I didn't realize he can sense fire the way my sister Rose does emotions. It makes sense now that I think about it, though. It's what makes his ability a psychic power, instead of something like Colin's Ravenguard abilities, which are more physical than mental.

Sometimes I wonder if I'll ever understand everything magic can do.

"I thought you were hunting with Colin," I say as Uncle Roy sets the tray onto the counter. His pale cheeks are tinged pink from the chilly weather, and he's dressed like a lumberjack in maroon flannel and khaki overalls that are almost too small for his bear-sized frame.

"Liam's in town for the day, so he took over. I've been putting up the holiday lights," he replies, shutting off the faucet. We both peer at the now goopy bread mess in the sink. "What happened?"

I shrug, glancing at the smoke-wreathed oven. "Nora said to take the bread out when it was done, but the timer hasn't even gone off yet. The house never burns anything. Do you think something's wrong with it?"

"I'm sure it's fine," he says. "It's probably just upset that Nora is leaving. And it always gets grumpier in the winter."

The house lets out a disgruntled rumbling sound, and the oven releases a burp of smoke straight into Roy's face.

He waves it away with an indignant sound. "What? You do!"

"I don't know," I say doubtfully. "Nora was just telling me—"

"Roy? I can't find my coat!" Aunt Elaine's voice captures Uncle Roy's attention, and he rolls his eyes at his sister. She's always misplacing things and blaming it on some faerie or another.

"It's under the bearded ax!" he calls back.

"Is that the Scottish one?"

"The Viking!" Uncle Roy says, exasperated. "I'm coming!"

He leaves as briskly as he arrived, abandoning me with the sponge masquerading as a challah loaf.

It's been like this for days now. The adults flying in and out of rooms, staying barely long enough to hold half a conversation before they're off again. Nora's been busy preparing for her trip, and Aunt Elaine and Uncle Roy have been out helping Colin with his Raven training. Even the twins have been holed up in their room, working on college applications and having the house deliver their food instead of eating in the ballroom with the rest of us. They're leaving tonight to tour the schools they're applying to, despite already having an unofficial scholarship offer from more than one.

So many things are changing, including me. I feel more a part of the Ravenfall Inn than ever; I'm even doing live readings with the guests now, *unsupervised*. With Gran, Nora, and the twins leaving, I'll get to do more than ever before, though the inn has been quiet as it always is around the end of the year. Most of our guests are drawn in by the Samhain celebration and blown out by the

7

early winter winds. It always grows unusually cold in Wick come December, the town's many shops and colorful homes topped in a layer of snow like a dusting of powdered sugar. The trees lose all their auburn leaves, the nights growing so thick it feels like you could scoop out an ebony handful.

Suffice to say, cold *and* spooky is a hard sell.

After relocating the challah-sponge to the trash—with no help from the house—I return to Colin's new journal and my now cold cup of Earl Grey and lay a hand on the nearest wall. "Are you okay?" I ask the house, but it's uncharacteristically silent.

Try as I might, I can't shake the feeling that something's off. I've never known the house to mess up like this, but Nora, Uncle Roy, and Aunt Elaine grew up here too. Surely they'd know if something is wrong.

I focus on the sketch of the Saint Knives. I've nearly finished the last of the details and the shading when a frantic voice trickles in through an open window.

"Max?" they call in that tone people reserve solely for the mischievous cat. "Max, no!"

My heart swells, and I leap to my feet and bolt for the front door, because I know that voice.

Henry is home.

CHAPTER 2

Colin

The Hollowthorn Woods are deathly quiet.

The scent of freshly turned earth mixes with something metallic in the chill morning air. We're close to our target. Close enough that my skin begins to prickle and my palms start to sweat as Liam and I continue down the frosted forest path, following a trail of iron-booted footprints.

"Tell me again," Liam instructs. He's walking a step ahead of me, the shoulders of his leather jacket beaded with morning dew. The fog has burned off, but the air still feels thick.

Viscous, I think. *Concentrated, not flowing freely.*

Thinking through the definitions of difficult words usually helps me stay calm on hunts, but this time, my throat still feels tight. "Unlike most fae creatures, redcaps won't die from iron," I say, running through the lesson Elaine gave me that morning before we started our hunt. "To survive, they have to kill and soak their caps in the blood of their victims."

A shiver runs through me at the thought. This is the same type of creature that once almost killed my mom. Apparently because of our magic, the blood of a Raven is even more potent and highly sought after by creatures like redcaps and vampires. As a teenager, Roy had tried to hunt one alone to prove he could be a Raven, too, and my mom had saved him. She'd fought three of them off by herself before help arrived but was badly wounded.

We're only after one, and I have Liam, but my stomach is still tied up in knots.

"And?" Liam presses, glancing back at me.

"And their weakness is other forms of magic," I say. "Like my Saint Knives. One cut, and they'll go up in flames."

"Which you do not want to touch."

"Which I do not want to touch," I repeat with a roll of my eyes. That part is obvious. Besides, this is the third time Liam has run me through this, and I'm getting tired of saying the same thing over and over again.

"And what do you do if—"

I cut him off with a groan, and he turns about to face me. At eighteen, he's several inches taller than me and much broader, but I'm starting to catch up. I grew nearly an inch this fall. I know because Anna keeps saying how unfair it is when she hasn't grown all year.

His expression makes him look just like Dad, and my heart

pangs at the thought. "This isn't a game, Colin," he says. "Redcaps are dangerous. You need to be prepared."

"I *am* prepared!" I summon my Saint Knives to prove it, their black and gold blades glinting in the dappled sunlight. With all my training the last couple months, they feel more natural in my hands than ever.

"There's more to being a Raven than stabbing things," Liam replies stiffly.

"I know that."

But Liam goes on. "You need to know everything you can about what you're hunting. Its strengths, its weaknesses, its behaviors."

"I know that too!" My hands curl around the knives. "I know what I'm doing. Stop treating me like a child."

Liam folds his arms. "Then stop acting like one."

My hands only close tighter. It's been like this every time Liam's been back lately. He takes over my training from Elaine and Roy and treats me like I don't know anything. As if I didn't just defeat the Irish King of the Dead and stop the veil to the Otherworld from dissolving.

With his help, an uncooperative voice reminds me.

Before I can come up with a good comeback, someone screams. Liam's eyes widen, and then we're both running down the path after the sound. Another scream pulls us deeper into the woods, and we burst into a wide clearing of frosted grass.

A pair of hikers are backing away from an advancing creature.

Short and thickset, with pointed ears and long, razor-sharp teeth, the redcap looks like a cross between an overgrown rat and a particularly grumpy gnome. Iron boots rise up to where the edges of its ragged tunic reach its knees, and in its clawed left hand it brandishes a pikestaff, which resembles an overly decorated spear.

Liam summons a handful of bluebell flowers from our parents' journal and begins to shake them. A deep, resonating hum spills across the clearing, and the redcap's ears twitch. Unable to resist the lure of the sound, it faces us, revealing a thin, sunken face with eyes as red as embers.

"Get the hikers to safety," Liam orders. "I'll handle this."

"But—"

"Now, Colin!" Tossing the bluebells aside, Liam summons a long dagger and launches himself at the redcap. The creature swings its pikestaff around, catching his blow, and I take the opening to duck to the hikers' sides, trying not to slip on the icy grass. I don't recognize them, which means they're most likely tourists, not Wick locals.

Which is probably why they're gaping at the redcap as if it's a statue come to life.

Returning my Saint Knives to the journal, I usher them back toward the trail they must have been following. "Hurry," I say when their horrified stares remain locked on the battle. "Run!"

The redcap lets out a terrifying screech as Liam's knife finds its mark, and it's enough to jolt the tourists out of their daze. They nearly trip over each other scrambling for the trail, and I run with them until it widens into the main path near the Faerie Garden in downtown Wick.

"What *was* that?" asks the woman. She's clutching the man's hand tight enough to make it leech of color.

I summon the last two glamour bags Rose made for me, each small and green like a medieval coin pouch. With the twins' focus on school, she hasn't had time to make more, and Liam and I have been going through them quickly.

I hold one out to each of them. "This will help."

They take the pouches, and I watch as they work their magic, the hikers' eyes growing unfocused and their faces slack. In a few moments, they'll think they ran into a mountain lion or a bear, not a vicious ancient faerie.

I retreat, not wanting to be here when the magic wears off, and fly back to the battle, thankful for the enhanced speed my Raven powers grant me.

When I arrive, Liam has the redcap pinned against a line of trees and bleeding from several cuts. But his knife is only iron, which won't kill a redcap without a mortal wound.

I summon one of my Saint Knives and send it flying.

The knife slices along the redcap's shoulder and buries into the trunk beyond, but that's all it takes. The redcap lets out a howl of frustration before it goes up in a whirl of smoke and flames that burn out almost instantly.

Only his iron boots and pikestaff remain.

I stare at them, a slow, creeping excitement welling up inside me. I did it! I actually did it! But when I turn to Liam, he's staring at me with obvious disappointment, and my excitement withers.

"I told you to leave this to me," he says, returning his dagger to the journal with a wave of his hand.

"I did what you said," I reply. "I got the hikers to safety. So what if I came back?"

"That's not the point, Colin." He runs a hand through his messy brown hair with a sigh. "If you can't listen to me when we're on hunts, then you shouldn't be going on them."

Iniquitous, I think, frustrated. *Unfair and morally wrong.*

The words bottle up in my throat and I only glare at Liam as he goes to gather the redcap's boots and weapon. Not long ago, I would have tried to force the emotions away. I'd have held my breath until my throat burned and I could control it, to prove that I could be strong. But now I let myself be angry.

All I wanted was to help. To protect people the way that I couldn't protect my parents. Because of me, those hikers are still alive, and there's one less redcap terrorizing Wick. Why can't Liam see that?

It's times like these that I really miss my parents. Mom always knew what to say to make me and Liam get along, and if she wasn't around, Dad would have us laughing about something in seconds, our fight forgotten. Now Liam and I are stuck with each other, arguments and all, and instead of the optimistic, fun-loving brother I remember, he's been grouchier than ever.

"This isn't over, boy."

The voice makes me jump and I whirl, searching for the source. There's no one there except me and Liam.

"I'll find you again, little Raven."

I shiver. The words had seemed as if they were right there, tickling my skin like a gust of wind, and I can *feel* something, like if I only reach out a hand, I'll—

"Colin?" Liam's voice brings me back to myself. I look around, but there's definitely nobody there, and now Liam's staring at me with furrowed brows. He's got the redcap's boots in one hand and the pikestaff in the other.

"Just thinking," I say curtly, still annoyed with him. The last thing I want is for him to suspect something's wrong on top of everything else. He'll stop taking me out on hunts if he thinks I'm hearing things.

The problem is, I *am*.

You inherited a sliver of my power, Fin Varra said that night on Samhain, and I fight back a shiver at the memory. The revelation that my family is descended from the Irish King of the Dead still hasn't quite settled. At the end of the battle, his ability to give and take life magic helped me bring Max back from the brink of death, but after that, I swore off using it, no matter how curious Elaine is to explore it.

I want nothing to do with the magic that killed my parents, or the being who did it, but I can't seem to get away from it. For weeks now I've been catching glimpses of spirits even the Ballinkays can't see. Elaine thinks I'm seeing into the Otherworld, but all I know is I'm tired of walking into a room I think is empty only to come face to face with an angry ghost. Even worse, I can feel Fin's magic inside me like a dam about to burst, just waiting for me to reach out and use it.

I just want it to go away.

Liam and I head back through the woods together, our shoes crunching atop a thick layer of dead leaves. He gives me the redcap's boots to carry, which are heavier than they look, and I try not to focus on the singed smell coming off of them. Once we're back at the inn, I'll dive into some magical research and forget all about the redcap's voice. The house has been making peppermint hot chocolate with snowflake marshmallows every night, and it sounds like just what I need right now.

I hold the shoes up for a better look. "Why are we bringing these back?"

"A redcap's boots and pikestaff can be used to birth a new redcap." Liam holds up a long, curved fang, which I hadn't noticed before. "Their fangs are also useful in a lot of medicinal practices. I thought Rose might want it."

When he visits, Liam spends almost as much time with Anna's older twin sisters as he does with me. They stay up late out by the firepits and go to the movies in town with Rose's girlfriend, ignoring me and Anna when we ask to go with them. Maybe tonight I'll ask Anna if *she* wants to go without *them*. It's been a while since we've done something fun together, just the two of us.

We emerge from Hollowthorn Woods into the grass fields surrounding Ravenfall. From the looks of it, Roy has been busy decorating while we were out. Blue and white holiday lights line the house's many mismatched dormers and eaves, flickering to the rhythm of one of the house's favorite classical songs, and garlands of holly and willow branches threaded with myrtle blossoms curl around the deck railing. Smoke puffs merrily from the chimney alongside the house's Santa hat.

"I'm heading out for another hunt tonight," Liam says as we approach the front driveway. "Do you know if Anna has finished your new journal yet?"

"She said she'd be done soon," I reply.

Over the last couple months, we transferred nearly everything from our parents' journal to my new one. Mostly information, fragments of mythology and entries about supernatural creatures gathered across generations of our family. Liam and I split the items stored inside it, each taking the ones we wanted, and Anna drew new images for them in my journal. Afterward, Elaine helped me create a magical link between the items and the journal, enabling me to store the items inside it and summon them when I need them, just like I do with the Saint Knives.

The knives are the last thing left to transfer over.

"You can probably take it with you the next time you visit," I say. "How long are you going to be gone?"

"Not sure." There's something off about Liam's voice when he says it, like he's nervous. Except Liam's never nervous. "I haven't seen my friend in a while, so we've got some catching up to do."

Now there's a pink flush to his cheeks, and I wonder if he's catching cold. He always acts like this when he talks about this friend, as if— "Wait, when you say *friend,* do you mean a *date*?" I demand.

Before Liam can answer, another voice shouts, "Max? Max, no!"

Relief spills across Liam's face as we hurry around the corner to find a small black cat batting something shiny across the gravel path with one tiny paw, a harried-looking man awkwardly chasing after him with a duffel bag in one hand. With olive skin, dark curls, and thick black glasses, he's practically a replica of the photos I've seen of Anna's older brother around the house, except a couple decades older and with a thick beard that'd give Roy's a run for its money.

My theory is confirmed when a moment later, Anna comes barreling down the stairs and shouts, "Henry!" a second before flinging herself into her dad's arms. He barely manages to catch her, still half-crouching after whatever Max has beneath his paws.

Max takes one look at them, then snatches up the object and bounds into the house.

CHAPTER 3

Anna

"**M**ax!" Henry yells again. "I'm sorry, Anna, I have to— Max!" He sets me down and takes off after Max into the house, duffel bag still in hand. I squash my disappointment. Usually, he spins me around until I'm a dizzy, giggling mess, already halfway through a story from his latest expedition before I even realize he's started.

My spirits lift when I spot Liam and Colin approaching, a spear-like weapon in Liam's hands and a pair of iron boots in Colin's.

"I guess you found the redcap?" I ask.

Colin hefts the boots. "Need any new shoes?"

I grin, but Liam gives his brother a disapproving look. "A redcap's boots are not a joke, Colin," he chastises as we climb the stairs to the deck together. "They're dangerous magical artifacts."

Annoyance floods Colin's face, and I whisper, "I thought it was funny."

He cracks a smile as we enter the house to the scent of pine and orange spice. A fifteen-foot Christmas tree takes up the entire corner to our left, bedecked in white faerie lights and gold ribbons, with a glowing star at the top. An elegant silver menorah with blue filigree sits in the window beside it, the candles placed and ready for Hanukkah.

As Colin sets the iron boots on the wooden bench inside the door, two kids clutching ice skates run past us up the stairs, on their way to the ice rink the house made out of the garden pond on the roof. Two elderly guests play a game of chess in the big bay window, and a young couple checks the inn schedule for the evening's movie that will be projected in the library. It's far quieter than it was at Samhain, and while I know Colin likes it better this way, I miss the rush of the holiday.

Henry's harried voice floats out from the kitchen. "Max, don't you dare!"

Colin and I exchange looks, then hurry into the kitchen to find Max dangling an ornate brass ring over the sink by one claw. Henry is creeping closer to make a grab for it, but Max's mischievous green eyes narrow, and he lets the ring drop into the garbage disposal. Henry makes a strangled sound and lunges for it—only for the ring to come flying back out a second later.

Henry snatches it out of the air, and Max lets out a low hiss at the house's interference. "Thank you," Henry tells the house with a sigh of relief. The house rumbles back a greeting, probably all too happy to thwart Max's plans. It's always liked my dad, who keeps his office organized and rarely uses the one computer inside it.

Max, on the other hand, is its mortal enemy, if mortal enemies bring you new hats to wear every day and fall asleep next to the coals of your fires.

"What was that about?" Liam asks from the doorway, still clutching the spear.

Henry holds up the ring. "This is a priceless magical artifact," he announces, before pointing at Max. "That is a cat. He— Oh, is that a pikestaff? Do you mind?" But Henry is already across the room, taking the pikestaff from a perplexed Liam and lifting it up to the light to inspect it.

"Fascinating," he says. "I've always theorized a redcap's magic stems not from its cap, but its staff, which is typically the cause of its victim's death."

Recognizing that he's about to go off on one of his rambling tangents, I quickly say, "Henry, this is Liam and Colin Pierce. The Ravens that Nora told you about."

Henry looks up from the staff, blinks owlishly, and says, "Oh yes, I almost forgot. Nice to meet you." He shakes Liam's hand, then reluctantly gives him back the pikestaff.

"What's that ring for?" Colin leans against the kitchen island. Max leaps up beside him and walks beneath his chin, his tail smacking Colin in the face. He bats it away, trying and failing to hide a smile.

With all the hunts they've been going on together the last

couple months, they've grown a lot closer, and Max spends almost every night in Colin's room now. It doesn't surprise me, since even though he looks like a cat, Max is really a Jabberwocky, a big, dragon-like creature that helps guard the Shield between our world and the Otherworld. Ravens and Jabberwockies have worked together for centuries, though usually they're bonded, the Jabberwocky sharing the Raven's magic so it can remain in the human world.

Max draws on the house's magic instead, though I've never known why.

Henry holds out the ring with a look of excitement. "This is a long-lost artifact known as the Seal of Solomon, a ring once worn by King Solomon of Israel thousands of years ago. It's said to grant the wearer the power to command demons and spirits."

The ring is thick, and I can just make out a pentagram engraved in the side. Henry taps the image with one finger and says, "This symbol is said to have given rise to the Star of David, and both the ring and Solomon occupy a large space in Jewish history and mythology."

"Does it have anything to do with Hanukkah?" I ask, thinking of the doomed challah loaf. The first night of Hanukkah is tomorrow, and even though my family isn't religious, we've always celebrated, cooking Jewish food and spending the night playing dreidel to win chocolate gelt (Kara always wins). This Hanukkah will be the first time we aren't all together as a family, what with Gran and Nora going to Ireland, and the twins setting off tonight on a school tour. Even my older brother isn't coming home from college.

Henry's fingers close over the ring. "Everything has something to do with everything, but the seal isn't a part of Hanukkah celebrations, no. But speaking of . . ." He crouches down by his duffel bag and pulls something free. "Your present!"

It's a blue and white sweater, stitched with snowflakes and Stars of David surrounding a cat wearing a kippah. Across the top it says *Happy Hanukcat.*

"I love it!" I take the sweater and hug it, the material soft and smelling of pine.

A look of longing crosses Colin's face, but before I can say anything, Liam checks his watch and asks, "Anna, do you know if your family is ready to go? I said I'd drop everyone off at the airport on my way out, but we're going to be cutting it close for their flights."

I shrug, nearly saying something about getting my family places on time being like herding cats, but Max is more on time than they ever are. "I think the twins are, but Nora is still packing, and Gran is—"

"Right here!" Gran sweeps in through the kitchen's side door, a fresh loaf of challah in hand and her suitcase levitating after her. Her auburn woolen dress reaches to her ankles, and her hair is dyed a bright blue and done up in a wild bun.

"I had a feeling you might be needing this," she tells me with a wink, setting the challah on the counter. Her bag drops to the ground with a *thunk,* the seams nearly bursting. Knowing Gran, she packed half her house in there.

I give her a hug, followed by Colin, before she kisses Henry and Liam each on the cheek. "I see your latest expedition was a success," she says with a nod to the ring.

Henry tucks it into the pocket of his shirt. "You won't believe where I found it. We were deep in—"

"I thought I heard a lecture starting." Nora enters the room, and I look away as she and Henry kiss. I make a face at Colin that breaks him out of his sullen mood. He makes a show of pretending to gag, and I grin.

"You're late," Nora says disapprovingly.

Henry winces, attempting an apologetic smile. "I got distracted by a new exhibit beside the airport for—"

"—ancient artifacts. Yes, I saw." Nora taps one temple, indicating she must have had a vision. "Except you were supposed to be here yesterday so we could all spend a night together."

Henry blinks. "Is today not Saturday?"

"Sunday," we all say together.

Henry mouths a silent *Oh* and offers Nora another remorseful grimace. She only shakes her head with an amused smile. They've been married nearly twenty years, and she's as used to his oddities as everyone else's in our family, just like he's used to hers.

"Just please try to focus on something *other* than magical objects while you're here," she teases.

My twin sisters appear in the doorway then, suitcases in hand.

Rose wears a flowing winter-green dress, her red curls spiraled atop her head, while Kara is in all black, looking like she just rolled out of bed with her blond hair in a messy knot. She takes one look at Henry coming toward them and slides her sweatshirt's hood over her head, turning her back to the kitchen and pulling out her phone.

Rose clasps her hands and glances between them, no doubt sensing both Kara's annoyance and Henry's disappointment. He gives Rose a hug, then Kara, who suffers it but doesn't return it.

"Is she upset or something?" Colin asks uncertainly.

"Kara and Henry don't really get along," I whisper. Then again, Kara and everyone don't really get along. Probably because she's part ogre.

"I heard that!" Kara calls without looking at us, and I stick my tongue out at her back. It's just like her to dip into everyone's minds with her telepathy when they're too busy chatting to notice.

Kara squeezes through the crowd over to the fridge, yanking it open to rummage inside. The house grumbles at the rough treatment, and I lean over the island next to Colin, thinking as loudly as I can, *Ogre, ogre, ogre.*

Kara's fingers tighten on the fridge until she finally whirls toward me and hisses so only we can hear, "He doesn't care about us, Anna. He's never here, and he never talks to us when he is."

My grin breaks. "That's not true," I say, clutching my new sweater close.

Kara rolls her eyes. "You wouldn't know. You worship him."

She slams the door and it comes flying back open, nearly clipping her shoulder. An apple leaps out of the drawer and into her hand before the door shuts grumpily once more.

"See, even the house thinks you're a jerk," I say, but Kara's already halfway back to the entry, clearly ignoring me.

Colin looks between us with a wince. "For what it's worth, he seems nice to me."

I smile. "That's because he is. Kara's the only one who doesn't get along with him."

Uncle Roy and Aunt Elaine join us then, and I squish closer to Colin. The kitchen turns into a chaotic flutter of greetings and goodbyes. Rose admires the redcap fang Liam hands her while Uncle Roy tries to convince Nora that the ruined challah loaf isn't his fault, and Aunt Elaine and Henry talk back and forth in rapid succession, no doubt discussing the Seal of Solomon. Gran levitates Kara's phone out of her hand to get her attention, but Kara snatches it back out of the air.

"Are you okay?" I ask when I notice Colin staring intently at the commotion.

He fiddles with his mom's Irish trinity knot necklace. He never takes it off, and I always catch him playing with it when he's lost in thought or seeking comfort. "I just wish Liam could stay a little longer."

"He'll be back soon," I say reassuringly, and Max bops his head against Colin's.

Gran joins us at the kitchen island. "I almost forgot, I brought you gifts."

I perk up as her bag unzips itself, allowing two small pouches to squeeze out. One lands in my outstretched palm, the other in Colin's. "Personalized tea blends. Anna-love, yours will calm doubts and enhance your openness, making it easier to use your powers. Colin, yours soothes hot emotions and rejuvenates the mind and body, which makes it the perfect post-training drink."

"One day you have to teach me how to do this," I say, opening my bag to sniff the tea. It smells of cardamom and vanilla.

"Come work with me at the tea shop this summer, and I'll do just that." Gran winks, and I throw my arms around her in a tight squeeze.

"I'll miss you while you're in Ireland," I say.

She hugs me back. "You'll be just fine, and we'll be back before you know it."

"Colin, Anna, come give me a hug!" Nora calls. We descend into the chaos of my family, each hugging Nora as the adults discuss car arrangements to get everyone to the airport.

"There are four of us," Kara says without looking up from her phone. "Liam's Charger can't fit us and our bags."

"It thinks of itself as much larger than that." Rose tilts her head toward a voice only she can hear. Her empathic abilities make it easy for her to read not only people's emotions, but also those of plants, animals, and objects. She doesn't get visions from them like me, just vague impressions.

"Actually, there's an expansion charm on the trunk," Liam says. "A witch friend of mine did it for me, so all your bags should fit."

Kara looks up suddenly from her phone, glaring at Liam. "I

did not overpack," she says, her telepathy clearly having picked up on one of his thoughts. Liam's face turns a dark shade of red, but Uncle Roy comes to his rescue.

"If you don't fit, we can take some people," he says. "Elaine and I need to go by the hardware store for a few things anyway."

Nora groans. "What did you break?"

"Nothing! Why do you always assume that?"

Aunt Elaine folds her arms. "Probably because you're always breaking things."

Nora gives them both an exasperated look. "Please don't burn down my inn while I'm gone, and, girls— Come back! Say good-bye to your father!" Kara and Rose are already halfway out the door. Rose circles back to give Henry a hug, but Kara throws up a half-hearted wave and continues out the front.

Liam gives the pikestaff to Henry and shakes his hand, then hugs Colin and me goodbye, ruffling Colin's hair until his brother smacks his hand away. Gran herds them all out with a sweep of her arms, the clatter of footsteps and scrape of suitcase wheels fading as they head outside.

Just like that, it's only me, Henry, Colin, and Max, who's eyeing the pocket Henry put the ring in. Henry doesn't seem to notice, his attention captured by the wooden chest from his office that I left sitting on the kitchen table. He strides over to it, running a finger along the carving of the hand symbol on its face.

"What's this doing in here?" he asks.

I set my new sweater on the island and join him. "I've been practicing my psychometry," I tell him proudly. "I can control when I get visions now after touching people, and I've started seeing other big moments besides death. But I'm still struggling with reading objects. I was hoping to be able to tell you something new about this one before you got home."

"Do you know what this is?" Henry asks as Colin joins us by the table, Max now perched on his shoulder.

I shake my head, and Henry taps the image of the hand. "This is called a *hamsa*. In Jewish mythology, it's a symbol that protects against evil. This chest was gifted to me by a Jewish witch. It's spelled to hold powerful magic."

"Could have used that on Samhain," Colin mutters.

Henry gives him a wry smile. "I can imagine. The way I heard it, the two of you had your hands full."

My heart sinks. "Did Nora already tell you everything?"

Henry gives me an apologetic look, and my disappointment only grows. I'd been hoping to recount our Samhain battle against the King of the Dead when he got home, knowing the story would keep him from disappearing into his office straightaway.

Colin knocks shoulders with me, then nods at my sketchbook, which is still open to the drawing of the Saint Knives. "Those look awesome. Are they done?"

I nod. "You just need to link the Saint Knives to it like you did the other items, then bond to the journal itself."

Henry picks up the journal. "This is truly fascinating. I've never seen a Raven's journal in person. I wonder if I might—" He cuts off at the sound of the front door swinging open. Setting down the journal, he pokes his head out of the kitchen.

"Did someone forget someth— Salem!" His voice pitches, and he disappears into the foyer. Curious, Colin and I follow, hovering in the doorway.

A man nearly the size of Uncle Roy is wiping his boots on the front mat, his tanned skin tinged pink from the cold. His size is intimidating enough, but with him dressed in a dark overcoat that reaches his knees, black combat boots, and all black clothes, I can't help but inch toward Colin—until the man's name clicks.

"Salem," I mutter, earning a quizzical look from Colin. I point at the new arrival and whisper, "He's a Raven."

And according to Henry, a really good one, though I've never seen him in action. We only met once when I was really young, and I remember thinking he was a giant. I still do.

"Henry," Salem says in a deep, rumbling voice. "Thank God you're here. I need your help."

CHAPTER 4

Colin

I gape at the massive man in the foyer, Anna's words on repeat in my head as he shakes hands with Henry. Like me and Liam, he's a Raven, a guardian of the supernatural world responsible for helping to maintain its balance. I've never met another one outside my family, partially because there are so few of us left, and also because until a couple months ago, I had no idea that I was one. My parents kept it a secret, hoping to keep me and my brother away from the magical world.

Looking at Salem, I feel like a poor imitation.

He's well over six feet tall, with broad shoulders and hands the size of dinner plates. His black hair is buzzed short, and a white scar cuts through the dark stubble along his jaw. It's not the only one; I spot several more on his knuckles and near his collarbone, and I can't help wondering how many creatures he's faced down.

He probably doesn't get sidelined by an overprotective older brother, I think irritably.

"My help?" Henry asks in surprise. "What do you mean?"

Salem runs a hand across the top of his head. "It's a long story. Can we sit?"

Henry glances at where we're peering around the door frame, then gestures for Salem to follow. "We can talk privately in my office."

They head past us down the hall, and a strange feeling prickles at the back of my neck. I sense something, but I can't quite . . .

Max lets out a low snarl from my shoulder, and I jump. If Salem notices, he doesn't turn, and I spot an ethereal shape fluttering by the stairs. The ghost of an old man waves at me once, then vanishes. Was Max growling at it or at Salem?

I glance at Anna to see if she saw the ghost, or if it's another only I can see, but she's staring at Salem's retreating back. She leans toward me to whisper, "Salem and my dad met on an expedition years ago. They used to go on them all the time together, but he only visited Ravenfall once a long time ago and I haven't seen him since."

"So what would make him suddenly come ask for Henry's help?" I ask.

Anna shrugs. "Let's go find out!" She grabs my hand and pulls me down the hall. The house masks our footsteps up to the study, and we each press an ear to the door, Max included.

"I swear you haven't aged a day," Henry is saying on the other side. There's the sound of compressing leather as Henry sits down at his desk. "It feels like just yesterday we were returning that stolen painting to the Edelstein family in the south of France."

Salem chuckles. "I wish this were that kind of visit."

"You said you needed help?"

There's a heavy sigh. Then Salem says, "According to a source of mine, a powerful demon is after the Tree of Life."

There's a clattering noise, as if someone dropped something in surprise. "The Tree of Life?" Henry repeats incredulously.

Anna gives me a quizzical look, and I whisper, "It's a sacred tree in a bunch of different cultures and religions. It's supposed to connect all forms of creation, including different realms, but that's all I really know. It's pretty obscure folklore. I only know something about it because Elaine reads the weirdest books."

"But why would a demon be after it?" she says at the same time Henry asks, "What does this demon want with the tree?"

"According to what I've read, the Tree of Life contains an untold power," Salem says grimly. "If one were to locate it and absorb its magic, they'd become like a god—immortal and incredibly powerful."

Anna and I exchange sour looks. We've had enough of ancient gods.

"That's not the worst of it, though," Salem continues. "If the tree is drained of power, the Otherworld will die, and magic along with it."

Anna gasps, and then the door flies open, sending me, her, and Max tumbling inside. We land in a heap on the thick rug covering the floor. A fire burns in the hearth, making the neatly organized but cluttered room feel cozy, bordering on cramped, with all five of us. For a moment I think Henry or Salem must have opened the door, except they're both sitting on opposite sides of Henry's desk. For some reason, the house revealed us.

"Thanks a lot," Anna mutters at the door as we pick ourselves up. The house grumbles back, sounding defeated, and Anna frowns.

Max takes one look at Salem, hisses, and bolts out the door. Salem laughs heartily. "Still hasn't forgiven me for stepping on his tail, I see."

"He probably never will." Anna rolls her eyes.

"Anna, Colin," Henry chastises. "Have you been listening this entire time?"

Anna gives him one of her terrible innocent smiles. "Define *entire*."

Henry groans, but a grin breaks across Salem's face. "Anna, look how much you've grown! I haven't seen you since you came up to my knee."

At that, Anna only sulks. "Not much has changed."

"You at least reach his waist now," I tease, and she sticks her tongue out at me.

Salem holds out a hand to me. "Salem Monroe," he says as I shake it, his hand dwarfing mine. "It's always a pleasure to meet a fellow Raven."

I start. "You knew?"

"I could sense you." Salem releases my hand. "I'd wager you could sense me too."

I think of the prickle at the back of my neck earlier. "I didn't know we could do that. I've never sensed anything around my brother."

Salem folds his arms with a nod. "That's to be expected. Auras between family members are usually very similar. It's like being used to your own scent."

Henry drags a hand down his face. "You knew they were there?"

Salem gives him a sheepish smile. "No harm in being curious."

"What are you going to do about the demon?" I ask, already running through what I've read about them over the last few months for my Raven training with Elaine. Different cultures call them different things, from the mazzikim in Jewish mythology that cause chaos in human lives to the Fomorians of the Irish seas. My parents' Raven journal has stories about a few they've faced: they all had different powers, appearances, and weaknesses.

No matter what kind of demon it is, though, if someone like that got ahold of the Tree of Life's power, it would be disastrous.

Salem looks imploringly to Henry. "That's why I'm here. According to my source, the demon after the tree is called Ashmedai."

Henry's eyes widen. "Ashmedai is the Jewish Lord of Demons."

Anna groans. "Great."

"Seconded," I mutter. Ancient powerful creatures are another thing I've had my fill of thanks to Fin, who tried to destroy the Shield to the Otherworld and merge the two realms. Now the Lord of Demons wants to take the power of the Tree of Life for himself so that he can rule over the realms, effectively destroying magic?

I groan too.

"Ashmedai is an extremely powerful demon," Salem continues. "He has a whole host of lesser demons under his command, and he's thousands of years old. Which is why I need your help to find and protect the tree before Ashmedai gets to it, Henry. If anyone can help me find it, it's you."

Henry fiddles with something in his pocket, then pulls it free, setting the Seal of Solomon on the desk. "I also have this."

Salem's eyes widen. "That ring will allow us to control Ashmedai if we encounter him. This should be a simple mission. What do you say, old friend?"

Henry scratches his beard, clearly torn. From what Anna's told me, this is the exact kind of adventure her dad loves, but it sounds dangerous too. Out of the corner of my eye, I see Anna's shoulders droop. She was so excited that her dad was coming home, and now it looks like he might be leaving again already.

Then Henry sighs. "I'm sorry, Salem, but I promised Nora that I would look after the inn and the kids."

Anna's head jerks up, a tentative smile curving her lips.

"Why don't they join us?" Salem glances at me. "I could use another set of capable hands against someone like Ashmedai, and the tree is hidden by a powerful natural defensive magic. Anna's ability may come in handy in locating it."

My excitement surges—and then dies at the uneasy look on

Henry's face. He's already shaking his head. "Ashmedai is known for his wrath. Nora would kill me if I put you in his path."

"A lot has changed while you were gone," Anna says quickly. "We defeated a god. We can handle finding a tree."

"Yeah, and we want to help," I say, already thinking about all the things I could learn from an experienced Raven like Salem. Liam only recently started hunting, and he hardly lets me do anything. If we help Salem, he can tell Liam all about it, and maybe next time my brother won't tell me to "wait here" while he does the heavy lifting.

Salem's mind must be in the same place because he adds, "It would be a great training opportunity for Colin, and I'd feel better having someone watching my back. Besides, we have the ring to protect us from Ashmedai."

"And we can finally spend some time together!" Anna presses her hands together in a pleading gesture. "Please? I've always wanted to go on an expedition with you."

Henry's reluctance begins to crack, but he puts up one last defense. "What about the inn? I promised your mother I'd take care of it while she was gone."

"Uncle Roy and Aunt Elaine are here," Anna says. "They can do it, right?"

The last of Henry's resolve crumbles. "Okay. We'll ask them, but if they say no, that's it."

We make our case to Elaine and Roy when they return from the hardware store later that afternoon. Neither looks impressed by our plan.

"You want us to do what?" Roy asks from his spot beside the fire. Anna and I sit on the library couches with them while Henry and Salem catch up out on the back porch. The mantel is wreathed in braids of holly and blue and white lilies, and the whole room smells lightly of cinnamon and cardamom. We're already halfway through a plate of gingerbread and maple cookies shaped as dreidels.

"Run the inn." Anna carefully enunciates each word, and I wince at her sarcasm. We're trying to convince Roy and Elaine, not make them mad. "You told Nora you wanted to be more involved, didn't you?"

Elaine gives her a flat stare. "Involved," she repeats. "Not in charge."

Anna seems to recognize her mistake, and quickly tries a new approach. "Please, Aunt Elaine? I've always wanted to go on an expedition with my dad, and it'll be great for Colin to learn from an experienced Raven. And you and Uncle Roy can try out running the inn for a while!"

"You *were* supposed to inherit it," Roy adds, earning a glower from his sister.

"It'll only be for a few days," I say, hoping to distract Elaine. "Just until we can make sure Ashmedai doesn't get anywhere near the tree."

Which, easier said than done. For all I know, this could take weeks, but I want to go more than anything. I *need* to, so I can show Liam what I'm capable of and make it clear to Roy and Elaine that I don't need the help of Fin's powers.

Roy twirls his fingers, making the fireplace flames spark and leap. The house scoots his couch aside a few inches in protest, and he stops. "I guess the inn won't be that busy for the next couple weeks," he says with a glower at the nearest wall.

"And I suppose you'll be safe with Salem," Elaine relents with a sigh. "His magical aura is one of the strongest I've seen for a Raven. Though let me tell you, he is *not* easy to read."

"And we'll have Max," Anna adds, the most important factor. As a Jabberwocky, his power's nothing to sneeze at.

"And this." I hold up the new journal. "Thanks to Anna, all the drawings are done. I just need to link the Saint Knives and then bond to it."

"All right, fine," Elaine says, trying and failing to hide her smile when Anna lets out a loud whoop of excitement. "But let's finish that journal first. You'll need it."

My fingers close tight around the journal, anticipation building in my stomach. I've been waiting for this moment for weeks now. Having my own journal brings me one step closer to being a real Raven, and another step farther away from Fin.

I nod. "Let's do it."

Elaine leans toward me over her knees. "Do you remember how to link an item?"

Standing, I lay the journal on the couch splayed open to the Saint Knives drawing. I summon the blades and set them on the pages. "First I focus on the link between me and the knives," I say. "Then instead of returning them to my parents' journal, I return them to my new one."

She nods, and I follow my own steps. It's a strange feeling, holding the magical link. It reminds me of the cord of magic that had strung between me and Fin Varra all those weeks ago on Samhain, connecting us. He'd used it to try and possess me, but the concept here is similar: the magic acts like a bridge, and I push the Saint Knives along it and into the new journal.

The image on the page glimmers, the pale golds of Anna's colored pencils turning almost metallic, the black deepening into midnight. Just like that, the knives are a part of the journal—and no longer accessible to me since I'm not bonded to the new journal.

Anna peers at the drawing with a crooked smile. "I nailed it."

"It looks even better than my parents'," I agree.

"Now it's time for you to bond to it," Roy says.

I take a deep breath. I'd known this was coming, but it feels even bigger now, and I don't want to mess it up.

"You'll need to break the bond with your parents' journal first," Elaine says gently. "Ravens can only link to one at a time."

I summon my parents' journal, running my thumb over the Irish trinity knot on the front, just like the symbol of my mother's necklace. Part of me is sad to be letting their journal go. It feels like giving up a piece of them, even though it'll just go back to Liam when we're finished, and most of the items and information in my new journal came from theirs. The other part of me is excited for what comes next. My very own Raven journal, my own adventures, and my own chances to protect people.

"What do I do?" I ask Elaine.

"Say the spell we used to bind you to it in the first place, but backward, and picture breaking the magical link between you and the journal," she replies. "Repeat after me."

She speaks slowly in Irish, and I repeat the words after her. As I talk, I imagine the bridge of power between me and the journal, the same way as when I build the link for a new item. As I reach the end of the sentence, I imagine snapping the bridge in half. I feel it come apart, like something clicking out of place. The trinity knot tattoo on my chest glows and then dissolves, the light trickling back into my parents' journal. Just like that, I can't sense it anymore.

It feels a lot like missing a piece of myself. I shiver, moving closer to the fire.

"Now for the new journal," Elaine says. "The old one was bound to your family's bloodline, and this one will be bound to yours. You'll need to place a drop of blood on the journal, then repeat the spell, building a new bridge as you go."

I think of the time in the motel when my parents' journal wouldn't let me open it, and only a drop of my blood had unsealed it. It makes sense that the same would be needed to create a bond between me and this new one.

I scratch a scab on the back of my hand from that morning's training, just enough to get a bit of blood on my fingertip. Then I press my finger to the journal. It's not leather like my parents', but a soft synthetic material that Anna decorated with a permanent marker. The outline of a raven with its wings thrown back, claws extended as if to land adorns the front, the inside done in an intricate series of lines with various Irish symbols, from a Triskelion covered in vines to the trinity knot from my parents' journal.

It's an ode to my family, my roots, and to Ravenfall.

Taking a deep breath, I repeat the words again, focusing on the new journal as I imagine a bridge of magic stretching between us. Like all those months ago, an effervescent feeling surges to life inside me. The raven symbol begins to glow, the light twirling up around my hands and wrists. The light dives into the spot above my heart, and when it fades away, the edges of a new tattoo poke up over my collar. I tug it down to see the raven symbol.

"Cool," Anna says with a grin.

I feel myself smile back, giddy with relief. I did it.

I have my own Raven journal.

Picking it up, I hold it close and look to Anna. "Let's go tell Henry and Salem we're ready."

CHAPTER 5

Anna

I barely sleep that night, my excitement leading to dreams of far-off places and camping underneath the stars with my dad. When I wake up, I jump straight into packing. Henry gave me one of his traveling backpacks, and I stuff it full of clothes, fluffy sweaters, and Gran's tea. Lastly, I add my sketchbook, where I've been taking notes on reading objects and drawing them in hopes of strengthening my connection to them.

I duck into my bathroom to get a toothbrush, and when I come back, my bag is on the floor, the contents scattered.

"You're acting like Max," I tell the house as I repack everything and set it back on the chair.

In response, the house locks my bedroom door.

I roll my eyes, though secretly it feels good to have the house react to me leaving like this. It only ever does stuff like this for Nora.

"I know you don't want to be alone with Uncle Roy and Aunt Elaine, but they're going to do great!" I grab my bag, edging toward the door. "Just give them a chance."

The house groans defeatedly.

I flip the lock and open the door, but something in my stomach tugs me into stopping. For all my teasing of Nora, I can't remember the last time I went on a trip. Leaving feels weird, but this is exactly what I've wanted for so long: to go on an expedition with Henry.

It's not a trip to Ireland, but as far as I'm concerned, it's better.

"It'll all be okay," I tell the house, patting the door frame. "We'll be back in no time."

It's late morning by the time I make it downstairs, where Colin, Salem, and Henry are gathered around the kitchen table over cups of hot chai, gingerbread pancakes, and thick slices of challah with homemade honey butter, all courtesy of the house.

There are shadows under Colin's eyes, a sign he's been up all night reading, probably about the Tree of Life and demons. He even brought his new Raven journal to the table with him, reviewing the notes he no doubt took. He keeps glancing at Salem out of the corner of his eye, as if waiting for him to comment on it, but he's deep in conversation with Henry over some old expedition they were on involving a Rusalka and near-death experiences.

I can't help but feel a little jealous at all the adventures they went on together. I've been asking my dad to take me on an expedition with him for years, and it feels weird listening to Salem, who's practically a stranger, talk like he knows my dad better than I do.

He probably does.

Henry's wearing a new necklace, the Seal of Solomon threaded through it, and he keeps playing with it while he talks.

Max watches both him and Salem from across the kitchen, having refused to join us for breakfast, his grudge still in full effect. Unless Salem apologizes for stepping on his tail, he'll probably never get over it, even if it was years ago. Still, I'm surprised he's not over there trying to steal Salem's food in retribution. It's almost as strange to me as the house exposing my eavesdropping last night. I still don't understand what happened, but I wonder if it has something to do with the burnt challah.

Aunt Elaine enters the room with an ancient-looking tome spread across her arms. "I found something you all might be interested in." She drops the dusty book onto the kitchen table, and the house rattles grumpily in response.

"Oh, I'll wipe it up after," she tells the house, pointing to the page she's on. "I think I found a way for you to locate the Tree of Life."

"Locate it?" I ask. "I thought something like that would stand out."

Salem chuckles. "The Otherworld is a very vast place. Without knowing where the tree is or having a way to find it, we could wander for years and never come near it."

"That," Aunt Elaine adds in her historian voice, "and the tree has a natural glamour barrier. You can only see the tree once you reach it. As you can imagine, that makes it very difficult to find, which is where the Myrtle Staff comes into play. It's said to have been created from the Tree of Life. If you can find this, Anna can use her psychometry to read its history and discover the location of the tree."

Henry leans back to get a better look at the book, which boasts a vague sketch of a staff that looks more like a tree branch. "I've heard of this staff. It enables the wielder to siphon the Tree of Life's magic. The Ravens of old deemed it too dangerous and locked it away in the Otherworld, a common practice with powerful magical artifacts that can't otherwise be destroyed. It keeps them from wreaking havoc in the human world."

"Do you think Ashmedai will be after it, too, then?" Colin asks, already copying the information down in his journal.

"I'm sure of it." Salem fiddles with a silver ring on his right hand. "Without the staff, Ashmedai won't be able to see through the tree's glamour or siphon its power. If we can get to the staff first, we can return it to the tree and make them one again."

I shuffle over to get a better look at the book. "I know the staff will help us find the tree, but how are we going to find the staff?"

"I think I know where to look." Salem pulls a small book out of his pocket, the leather front engraved with the silhouette of a howling hound.

Colin perks up immediately. "Is that your Raven journal?"

"Sure is," Salem says with an easy smile. He flips open to a yellowed page, the writing in fancy cursive. "My parents always said our family is one of the oldest Ravenguard lines in existence and that Ravens of our line were responsible for sealing away a lot of magical artifacts in the Otherworld. It's partly where I got my interest in them, and why Henry and I became friends when we met on that expedition years ago."

He points to a sketch of what looks like a series of caves. "We call this the Crypt."

"That's inviting," Aunt Elaine mutters.

"It's the Otherworld," Salem says with a laugh. "Point is, it's said to contain a lot of sealed magical objects. It's a collection of caves protected by powerful magic. Legend has it that you have to complete a series of tests to access it."

"How fascinating!" Henry says excitedly.

I make a face. Tests and studying and research are not my style, but Colin is practically vibrating with excitement in his seat. It's the most animated I've ever seen him. Then again, seeing as he's normally so quiet and reserved he might as well have disappeared into one of his books, I guess any change is a big one.

"It should take us a couple of days to reach the caves, and then a few more to reach the Tree of Life and return the staff." Salem tucks away his journal. "If all goes according to plan, we shouldn't be gone more than a week."

Aunt Elaine picks up her book and snaps it shut. "I expect you to keep them safe, Salem," she warns.

"I will," he assures her, but rather than look convinced, Aunt Elaine's brow furrows.

"Why am I having such a hard time reading your aura?" she asks.

"Ah." Salem holds up a hand, where a simple gold band encircles one finger, next to another silver ring. "The gold one is spelled to prevent psychic abilities such as empathy and aura reading from working on me. I've found in my line of work it helps if the things you're after don't have a leg up on you. After all, psychics aren't the only ones with those kinds of powers."

I think of Fin, who was able to find Colin even when he was warded, thanks to their bond. A ring like that would have been really useful back then.

The kitchen's side door swings open, and Uncle Roy enters. "I've put all of your packs out on the deck," he says, dusting off his hands. "Are you all sure about this?"

"We'll be fine," Salem assures him, laying a hand on Colin's shoulder. "Between the two of us, we can handle anything."

Colin practically beams at that, and I wonder how excited he is about having another Raven around. He talked about Salem practically the entire night last night, in between reading up on the tree and practicing with his new Raven journal.

Meanwhile, I spent the evening trying to read the chest carved with the hamsa and failing miserably. It just doesn't want to talk, or maybe I'll never get better at reading objects. What if I can't read the Myrtle Staff either? Then we'll never find the Tree of Life, and all of magic could be at risk.

I'll figure it out, I tell myself. Just like I did my other visions. This is my chance to show my dad what I've learned, and really put my new skills to the test. Maybe then he won't be so reluctant to take me on expeditions, and we can spend every night talking about magical artifacts.

We eat the last of our breakfast and then finish packing. It's just after noon by the time we each grab a slice of pecan pie from the counter and head for the side deck where our packs are gathered.

Aunt Elaine pulls Colin aside at the kitchen door, and I join them while the others go on ahead. "You know," she begins, "if you're going into the Otherworld, Fin's magic may come in handy. I think you should reconsider your decision not to use it."

Colin's face darkens. "I don't want anything to do with it."

"He was the King of the Dead, Colin. You can't just ignore a power like that."

"Watch me." Colin ducks out onto the deck, and I give Aunt Elaine a sympathetic shrug.

She frowns at his retreating back. "Keep an eye on him, Anna. He might be acting like everything's okay, but he's dealing with a lot. He can only suppress magic like that for so long before it starts acting out on its own."

I give her a mock salute, though inside I'm just as worried. The power to manipulate life magic, his connection to the Otherworld—they're not normal abilities for a Raven, and we don't know the extent of what he can do with them since he refuses to even try them out.

"Be nice to the house while I'm gone," I say, and join the others on the deck.

Henry, Salem, and Colin have each slung a large pack over their shoulders, while I take my smaller one. As we descend the back stairs, Max sprints down the outdoor staircase from the roof, having finished switching the house's Santa hat out for a kippah for the first night of Hanukkah tonight. He drops the Santa hat inside, then bounds over, clambering onto Colin's shoulder as we cross the grass field into Hollowthorn Woods, where the massive oak tree we call Grandpa waits.

"Promise us you'll be careful," Aunt Elaine says worriedly.

Uncle Roy slings an arm over her shoulder. "They'll be fine! I'm just jealous we're not going too."

"Honestly, I'd say you have the more difficult of the two jobs," Henry says, and Uncle Roy's smile falters.

Salem looks to Colin. "Do you know what we need in order to travel to the Otherworld?"

Colin holds out a hand, then summons a wooden amulet with an engraving of a sprawling tree on it. "My brother used one of these to cross into the Otherworld."

"It's a Tree of Life amulet," Henry notes with obvious fascination. "Most Ravens have one. Fitting for this trip."

"Do we all need one?" I ask, but Henry shakes his head.

"One should be enough to get us all through since we're together," he says. "We just need to open a portal, which is where Grandpa comes in. The amulet will allow us to stay in the Otherworld."

Colin cranes his head to look at Max perched on his shoulder. "Could Max transport us too? Like he does with spirits?"

"It would take almost all of his energy to do so, but yes," Salem replies. "Jabberwockies are creatures of the Shield and capable of helping things cross over."

Max lifts his head proudly, and I give him a pat.

We each set our pieces of pie down before Grandpa. "Will you take us to the Otherworld, please?" I ask.

The tree's leaves rustle, and then the trunk spirals apart, revealing a dark cavern. The last time I traveled this way, Colin and I were on our way into downtown Wick to track down Fin Varra's second in command. Now we're chasing a demon through the Otherworld.

Colin knocks shoulders with me, his smile telling me he's thinking the same thing. "Embrace the weird," he says, and I grin.

Then we dive into the tree.

Traveling through the portal is always a little disorienting, but this time, when the world turns upside down and the sky stretches out beneath us—it just stops. We stay that way, with our feet rooted to the green earth, the stars like a pool of fireflies beneath us.

I make a noise of surprise and grab Colin's arm, who's staring around in bewilderment. Max clings to his shoulders for dear life.

"What's happening?" Colin asks. "Aren't things supposed to turn the right way up again?"

"Ah, so you've traveled this way before," says Henry with

delight. "I'm sure you glimpsed this realm that time. This is the Otherworld."

"So we're just going to be upside down the *entire time*?" I ask, already beginning to feel the blood rush to my head.

Salem shakes his head. "Just give yourself a moment to adjust. Accept the strangeness instead of trying to correct it."

"Embrace the weird," I mutter, exchanging nauseated looks with Colin. We both take a deep breath, and I try to make myself relax, which isn't easy when you're dangling upside down over a magical realm. But eventually, my perspective begins to shift.

One moment I'm staring down at an endless sky—the next I'm looking up at it. I drop my gaze to the horizon to find Hollowthorn Woods stretching out before me.

"It looks exactly the same as home!" I exclaim.

Colin blinks a few times, Max now settled safely back around his neck. "It feels different, though. The air is thick with magic."

I take a moment to focus on the woods, waving a hand through the air. It feels almost like moving it through water. Other than that, you wouldn't know we'd gone anywhere. The oak trees around us are the same shade of winter brown, the grass a lush green beneath our feet, all of it dusted with a thin layer of snow and frost. Only the sky is dark and full of stars, when it'd been just after noon when we left Ravenfall.

"Hollowthorn Woods is more than just a weak spot in the Shield," Henry explains. "It's one of many powerful sources of magic that exist in both the human world and Otherworld. It'll look much the same in many places, but just as many will be strange and unfamiliar."

"I thought there'd be spirits and monsters," I say, half expecting to find grinning fae and hungry vampires around every tree.

Salem gives a light chuckle. "Oh, they're here."

"They likely stay away from the area the house occupies." Henry nods to a nearby clearing like the one outside Ravenfall. The grass is indented as if something large sits on it, though there's no house there.

Picking up a stick, Henry draws a line in the wet dirt. "Think of it this way. The human world is here." He points above the line. "The Otherworld is here." He points below. "They're mirrors of each other, but just like when you look at yourself in a mirror, you look different than in a photograph because of the angle you're reflected back at. So, too, does the Otherworld differ from ours."

He draws a series of boxes in the bottom half of the diagram. "Think of it as several dimensions crammed into one, each one full of magic and mystery and home to many creatures and places of myth. It's a truly delightful place to explore."

Colin leans in close to me. "I think your dad needs to check his definition of 'delightful.'"

"It's the Ballinkay version," I whisper back.

Henry jabs his stick upright in the earth. "Any questions?"

Colin raises his hand. "Why is it dark here?"

"Time is different in the Otherworld," Salem replies, already alert and surveying the area. "Night is day, and day is night, though it's not a direct correlation. In my experience, the Otherworld is ahead of the normal world. Since it was afternoon when we left, I suspect it's a couple hours before sunrise here."

"Does that mean it's the morning after the first night of Hanukkah?" I ask Henry, who nods.

"Hanukkah Sameach!" he says merrily, and I grin back at him, though I wish we had a menorah to light. I always like listening to him read the Hebrew blessings as we light the candles, even if I'm not sure what they mean. I do know it's supposed to be lit at sundown, though, so technically we're way past the right time, but we've never been great at technicallys.

Salem sets down his pack. "Since it's safer to travel in the daylight, let's set up camp here for the next few hours and get started on our journey after sunrise."

At that, Colin looks relieved. "I could use a nap."

"Best you stay awake," Salem tells him. "It's only a couple hours until dawn, and it'll help you sync up with the time here."

Colin groans but doesn't protest further, and we take the next couple hours to rest and explore the immediate area. Henry points out all types of flowers with names I've never heard of—and seeing as Rose made it her personal mission to teach me as many as possible, that's saying something. It turns out they're all magical varieties that only grow in the Otherworld, including an adelflower, whose icy-blue bulblike tops light up when danger is near.

Max bats at them like cat toys, making the bulbs flicker on and off. Unlike the rest of us, he actually looks different in the

Otherworld. Healthier and fuller, like a flower that's finally gotten enough sun.

"Jabberwockies are creatures made of magical energy," Henry says when I mention it. "This place was his home once before he came to the human world. He's probably feeding off the magic here."

I pepper him with more questions, just happy to hear his voice again after so long. For years, I've wanted to go on one of his expeditions with him, and now that we're finally doing it, I feel lighter than air.

"Effervescent," I mutter, thinking of a word Colin taught me months ago. *Bubbly. Light.*

"Hmm?" Henry glances up from inspecting a gold and red mushroom. While he's looking away, it pulls up three stubby legs and scurries into the tall grass.

"Nothing." I grin, pointing at the hole it left behind. "Your mushroom ran away."

By the time the sun begins to rise, I've bundled up in my new Hanukcat sweatshirt, plus a thick black coat with a fuzzy lining. Meanwhile, Colin is only wearing his usual red and black flannel over a gray T-shirt with black jeans, as if it isn't near freezing.

"Stupid Raven powers," I mutter, wishing I had heightened physical abilities too.

Colin doesn't hear me, his attention turned inward. He keeps twisting his head to look over his shoulder, as if expecting to find something creeping up behind him. I wonder if he's sensing spirits, since Fin's powers connect him to the dead. Even back at Ravenfall, he could see ghosts my family couldn't.

"Is it you know what?" I ask him quietly.

He stiffens, eyes snapping to Salem to make sure he didn't hear. "It's nothing."

"But—"

"I don't want to talk about it, Anna," he hisses, and I deflate. It's not the first time Colin's been grumpier than usual lately, but it still makes me want to put faerie dust in his socks and wish for itchy toes.

Salem glances at the brightening sky, then pulls his Raven journal from a pocket. "All right. According to my journal's information, we head west until we hit the Gemstone Forest, and then follow that to the Pishon River."

"The first river," Henry mutters to himself.

"From there, we'll locate the Crypt, retrieve the Myrtle Staff, and return it to the Tree of Life before Ashmedai finds us." Salem snaps the book shut. "Let's head out."

CHAPTER 6

Colin

The Hollowthorn Woods on this side of the veil are everything Henry said they'd be. At first glance, they look just
like the trees Liam and I were hiking through yesterday morning: thick-trunked with gray-green leaves and sprawling branches
dusted with snow. But when I'm not staring at them head-on, I
see them rustling and moving as if greeting each other, or else
shaking free the snow with the same displeasure the house shows
a messy room.

Even on the human world side, the Hollowthorn trees had
been more than greenery: here, they're alive, and I can't help feeling like we're being watched.

"Hello, little Raven."

I start at the redcap's voice, trying to find him, but I don't see
anyone. Salem gives me an odd look, and I pretend to swat away
a bug to cover up my reaction. I'd worried Fin's power would be

stronger in the Otherworld, and sure enough I can feel it sitting in my chest like a stone, a well of magic waiting to be accessed.

I try my best to ignore it, but it's hard when I can practically feel the spirits around us.

"I told you I'd find you again," the redcap's voice whispers. It floats over my shoulder like the buzz of a gnat, refusing to be swatted away. *"You're in my world, now."*

"And you're dead," I mutter, and imagine squashing Fin's power down into some dark pit inside me. When only silence answers, I let out a breath. As long as I don't let Fin's magic in, I can control it, and eventually, maybe suppress it. It's just like any other magical training; I just have to practice.

We walk for miles, following Salem's directions toward the Gemstone Forest and passing one strange thing after the next. A haunting melody emanates from a small, sapphire blue pond, but when we stop to investigate, we realize the sound is coming *from the water itself* and hurry onward. We pass through an arch of branches, where the trees on each side of the path have grown together to form a tunnel. Eyes of every color watch us from the branches' shadows, until we come upon a silent crow perched on a low-hanging branch. It transforms into a pitch-dark hare before our eyes.

Salem takes one look at it and summons an iron knife, and the creature disperses in a puff of black smoke.

Uncanny, I think. *Mysterious, unsettling. Strange.*

Yet also kind of beautiful. The whole place is steeped in magic so thick I feel like I'm breathing it in with every lungful, and I can't help wondering what's behind each tree or around the next bend. Everyone made the Otherworld sound like such a terrifying place, but so far, it just seems different.

"And that's how I ended up riding a kelpie across Loch Ness, arriving just in time to break the witch's spell," Salem says, concluding the latest of the Raven adventure stories he's been sharing with me for the past couple hours.

On my shoulders, Max lets out a little snort. He hasn't left his spot, and my neck is sore and stiff from balancing him and craning to look up at Salem, but I can't stop staring. Each of his stories is more impressive than the last, from taking on nests of vampires to chasing off a wyvern that'd been terrorizing a remote mountain town.

"You've saved so many people," I say, fiddling with my mom's trinity knot necklace. "I've barely done anything."

Over the last couple months, Elaine, Roy, and Liam helped me a lot with my Raven training, but other than the redcap, I've only helped take down one wraith and relocated a particularly nasty cluster of gnomes from Rose's girlfriend's garden. There had been a couple others, but Liam made me stay home while he dealt with them.

"I want to do more," I tell him. "But my brother won't let me."

Salem gives me an understanding look. "My parents were the same way. They thought if they kept me away from the Raven life, I'd be safe. But people like us are always targets by nature of what we are. We need to be prepared to defend ourselves. Besides, it's our duty to use our abilities to protect others."

"That's how I feel, but my brother won't listen." I kick a pebble, sending it scattering into the nearby underbrush. It comes flying back out, and I duck.

"Best not to anger the vegetation!" Henry calls from where he and Anna lag behind us. Not for the first time, we slow down to let them catch up. A part of me wishes they'd hurry. The sooner we reach the Crypt, the sooner we can return the staff to the Tree of Life and put a stop to Ashmedai's plans.

Salem studies me intently. "Well, if your brother won't help you achieve your goal, I will."

"Really?" I lift my head.

He nods, a smile brightening his green eyes. "We'll spend our evenings training and go on a few hunts while we're here. That way, the next time you see your brother, even he won't be able to deny you're ready to be a full-fledged Raven."

A full-fledged Raven.

No more taking orders from Liam or being told to let someone else handle it. I could take my own missions, fight my own battles.

I could be like Salem, and actually *help* people, the way I couldn't help my parents.

I only realize I've been grinning at Salem this whole time when Anna's misery-filled voice asks, "Haven't we passed that tree before?" She gestures at a towering willow, one of the few intermixed among the oaks. I recognize it because she pointed out the big knot in the center that looks like an eye the last time we passed.

We slow, surveying the small clearing. "It's definitely the same place," Henry says, scratching his beard. "How did we manage that?"

A strange feeling comes over me then, like a shift in air pressure. Salem steps closer to me. "Do you sense that too?" he asks.

I nod. There's something here.

"Feel what?" Henry asks as Anna nervously scoots closer to him.

Salem presses a finger to his lips and summons a curved sword to his hand. I do the same with my Saint Knives, putting my back to his so we can see every angle. I hadn't noticed it before, too enthralled in Salem's story, but there's something strange about the trees here. Out of the corner of my eye, I swear I see colorful shadows thrown against their trunks. But when I face them head-on, they look their normal grayish brown.

Max leaps down from my shoulders, sniffing the air. I expect him to growl, but he only sits down on his haunches, his tail flicking lazily.

The colorful lights play across the trees again, and I lift my knives just as Salem whispers, "There."

One moment there's nothing, and then the next I see it: beneath the boughs of the willow tree lies a large lupine creature with a coat of many colors. They swirl and run into each other, spring greens and buttermilk yellows, burnt copper and sunset reds. The longer I stare, the more the colors move, until I forget the feel of my knives and the towering presence of Salem at my back.

Something snaps, startling me, and I blink several times to find Anna standing in front of me. She snaps her fingers again for good measure.

"I'm okay," I say.

"Henry says not to look directly at it," she tells me.

"What *is* it?"

"A beast," Salem growls. "It's hypnotizing us with some sort of glamour."

Henry readjusts his glasses, peering harder at the creature despite his advice. "I think it's a defense mechanism for when it sleeps. It keeps other creatures from getting too close by trapping them in a loop outside its radius. I suspect that if we'd been trying to veer out instead of in, we would have escaped it and continued on our way."

"Suspicion isn't certainty." Salem adjusts his grip on his knife. "It could just as easily be using this ability to trap prey."

From what I know of the magical creatures that populate the Otherworld, Salem's explanation sounds far more likely. Liam barely survived being here for two weeks before Samhain, and Fin and his people had been desperate to escape it. No matter how innocent the veneer, I know this place is dangerous.

"What should we do?" I ask.

"Why don't we try going around again?" Anna suggests, but Salem shakes his head.

"We shouldn't expose our backs to it." He hefts his blade. "We'll deal with it here and now."

I shift my grip on my Saint Knives, ready to guard his back.

As if sensing our intent, a ripple courses through the creature's body, and it slowly unwinds. An angular head lifts from the ground, its short, round ears twitching intently. With a long, slow stretch, it rises to its massive paws, a short, shaggy tail flicking side to side. The colors in its coat undulate with every movement, and I have to focus not to get caught up in them again.

"Oh my," Henry breathes. "I know what that is. It's the Tzavua, a beast of Jewish mythology whose coat is said to contain three hundred and sixty-five colors."

"I've read of it," Salem says warily. "It's some sort of hyena demon."

Henry tilts his head to the side. "I think that's a misconception." But Salem is already approaching the beast, his sword raised. I move after him, filtering out Henry's calls for us to wait.

The Tzavua sniffs the air—then its bright, golden eyes slowly darken to black. What was once a waist-high creature begins to stretch upward and outward, the colors in its coat growing brighter and more agitated, until it's nearly as tall as the willow tree under which it slumbered.

"Colin," Anna calls. "Be careful!"

I falter, unsure of how to fight something so large, but when Salem refuses to back down, I take a deep breath and go with him. He's giving me the chance to prove myself, a chance Liam never would, and I don't want to disappoint him.

A shape goes flying past me, and I pause as Max bounds up

to the Tzavua. He looks impossibly small beside it, no larger than one of the creature's toes. Still, the Tzavua acknowledges him, bending down its head as he stretches toward it.

Between one blink and another, I see a different Max. One moment, he's the small black cat. The next, he's in his Jabberwocky form, long and dragon-like with leathery wings and big, curving claws—except he's nearly the size of the Tzavua. Then he's himself again, and the two of them are sniffing noses like dogs passing on the street.

We all watch in tense silence, Salem's grip tightening on his blade. Their interaction feels like an apology, and if the Tzavua doesn't accept it, then we're about to find out really quick just how dangerous the Otherworld can be.

Suddenly the Tzavua lets out a dismissive snort that sounds like a thunderclap, then shrinks bit by bit back to its normal size, curls up among the roots of the tree, and goes back to sleep. Max bows to it, backing away slowly. The moment he's outside the boughs of the willow, the image of the Tzavua fades like a mirage.

Max bounds back to me, clambering up to my shoulder.

"Are you friends with that thing?" I ask him, and he shrugs.

Henry readjusts his glasses, looking at the spot where the Tzavua had been. "I think we've been forgiven for trespassing."

"Good thing," I mutter, not entirely sure even two Ravens and a Jabberwocky are enough to take on something like that.

Salem summons away his sword and readjusts his pack. "Let's go," he says gruffly. "Before it wakes up again."

CHAPTER 7

Anna

Before long, I've bundled a bright blue scarf that Rose knitted me about my neck, added a pair of woolen gloves, and stuffed all my curls into a beanie until my head looks like lumpy dough. Walking is helping, but now my feet have begun to complain, and I'm already bored. It's been quiet since we ran into the Tzavua, and Salem and Colin are on even higher alert than before.

When I find myself walking alongside Salem, my boredom and curiosity get the better of me and I ask, "So, where've you've been lately?"

I haven't seen him for almost seven years, since he visited Ravenfall after his first expedition with my dad, and I can't imagine he was on the list of Ravens that Nora called to warn about Fin during Samhain. If Salem had known about Fin and his wraiths, he'd probably have come rushing to help no matter what Nora said. I know my dad and Salem have been on more expeditions together since that first one, though. Salem has a thing for magical objects too.

"Traveling," Salem replies.

I wait, but he doesn't say anything else, so I press, "Where did you go?"

"A lot of places."

Again I wait, and again he just keeps walking, his head on a constant swivel. I look with him, searching for some kind of threat in the thick bundles of trees—a set of eyes, the curve of a claw—but the wood is surprisingly quiet and unthreatening.

Maybe that's what's got him nervous.

Still, he could at least give me a real answer. I start to ask another question when Salem perks up as if he's heard something. His stride lengthens, carrying him swiftly away from me. I glower at his back, slowing until I'm walking beside Colin again.

"I don't remember him being such a grouch," I grumble.

Colin gives me a knowing look. "How many questions did you ask him?"

"I didn't—" I cut off with a grimace. "Only two, but he was giving me the worst answers."

"Not everyone wants to be interrogated," he says. "Salem's reticent."

"Ah, yes, reticent. That word. Which means things."

He rolls his eyes. "It means he doesn't talk about things very easily."

"Who do I know like that?" I mutter, earning a glower from

Colin. I give him an innocent smile, but that only makes him glare harder.

I throw up my hands. "What? You're even grouchier than him lately!"

"Well, then, maybe I should walk with him." Colin jogs to catch up with Salem, leaving me stranded between them and Henry, feeling foolish. Maybe that *wasn't* the best thing to say. It wouldn't be the first time my mouth got me into trouble, but it's not usually with Colin, not anymore.

At first, I always said the wrong thing around him, not considering how unused he was to the magical world. But eventually, I got better at thinking before speaking, and he decided he liked my honesty. Ever since he started going on hunts with Liam, though, he's been grumpier than the house when Kara blasts music all day.

By the time we set up camp for the night, my feet are sore and aching. We found a small, protected clearing up against a hill free of snow, where the trees ring like chimes when the wind blows through them. Salem set up four identical lantern-like objects around the area, explaining that they're spelled to create wards inside their perimeter.

I try not to think about the types of things lurking in the woods that require us to have wards.

Collapsing onto my rolled out sleeping bag, I don't move again until Henry hands me a bowl of matzah ball soup from our cook-fire, which I devour. Apparently, his travel pack is spelled with an expansion charm like the trunk of Liam's Charger, and the house made us a whole bunch of food to take with us. All thankfully unburnt, though the challah is a little underbaked, but I like the chewiness.

"Dinner's ready!" Henry calls to where Salem and Colin are training beneath the branches of a sprawling oak. Salem has been showing Colin a new way to hold his Saint Knives, enabling him to better attack and defend simultaneously, and they've been going at it since we stopped. Max sits nearby, watching every move.

I wish I had even a fraction of their energy. With their Raven powers, they have enhanced speed, strength, and senses, making an all-day hike seem like nothing to them. I, on the other hand, am doing my best imitation of a puddle of Jell-O. I could really use one of the house's fires and a warm cup of peppermint hot chocolate right about now, but I keep that to myself. I don't want Henry thinking I'm not cut out for his expeditions.

"Just a few more minutes!" Colin replies. It's always just a few more minutes with him and training. If it weren't for Nora, I'm pretty sure he'd sleep out in the grass field behind the house. Actually, he *has* fallen asleep in the library while studying more than once, much to the house's dismay.

Despite announcing dinner, Henry barely touches his bowl. He's already wrapped up in a book he packed for the trip, and the only sounds are of Colin and Salem training and me slurping down soup.

I try not to let it feel awkward, but the truth is, sometimes that's the only thing I feel around my dad. With how often he's gone, and how much time he spends in his study when he's home,

I've never felt as close with him as I do with Nora and the rest of my family.

He doesn't care about us, Kara's voice reminds me, somehow twice as vicious in my memory. It sparks an angry tightness in my chest. I know Henry cares about us—he's just busy—but I still wish trying to think of something to say to him didn't feel like trying to speak another language.

Sometimes it seems like the only time he talks to me is when he's teaching me something about magical objects.

Feeling miserable, I pour myself a cup of the tea Gran brought me using the hot water over the fire. The cardamom and vanilla scent envelop me in a warm hug, and I sip the earthy tea. Its effects set in almost immediately, the edges of my doubt wearing away and making room for something else.

An idea occurs to me, and I set down the mug. If magical objects are what my dad loves, then maybe I can use them to get closer to him. I might not have been able to read that chest with the hamsa on it, but I've managed to read other things. If I can learn how to do it well, Henry and I will have a lot more to talk about.

Besides, we're getting close to the staff, and I need to make sure that when we find it, I can read it. Otherwise, we'll never get to the Tree of Life before Ashmedai finds us.

"Can I see your watch?" I ask Henry.

He takes it off and hands it to me without looking up from his book. I cup it in my palms, the metal still warm from his skin. With a simple, round face and an aged leather band, it hardly looks like anything special, but my dad has worn it every day for as far back as I can remember. It's as much a part of my image of him as his beard and glasses.

Taking a deep breath, I try to relax, letting my magic flow naturally like Nora taught me. I can feel it like a lazy river inside me, coasting through my arms and legs and chest. Now I just need to build a bridge between myself and the watch. I picture the bridge forming, imagining the magic as a bright light like the Shield when it materializes, and direct it to the watch.

But just like the chest, the magic refuses to take root, and my mental hold on it slips.

"Careful," Henry warns. "That watch is pretty delicate."

I realize I've locked my hands around it in fists and relax them. "Sorry. I'm having trouble reading it."

Henry closes his book and scoots a little closer. "How exactly does reading an object work?"

I explain my technique and he nods along until I finish. "I wonder.. . . Well, it's a lot easier to build bridges with people, because you know them, right?"

"Even strangers," I say. "I might not know them well, but I can still tell when someone's nervous, or kind."

"Perhaps doing the same with the objects will help." Henry holds out his hand for the watch, and I give it back. He turns it over, showing me the engraved initials on the back: *HS.*

"This was my father's watch," he explains. "He made it himself and engraved his initials on the back: *Henry Stern.* I'm the second Henry in our family, and your brother is the third. My father always thought it strange that I took your mother's last name, but in time he came to realize that nothing about the Ballinkays is traditional."

A faint smile pulls at his lips, and I lean closer, already enthralled by his story. "He gave me this watch the day your mother and I got married. I'd barely had it on for an hour before my father and I were arguing again, something we did a lot. I ended up throwing the watch. The glass face broke, but the next morning I found it outside my door, completely repaired."

"What were you and Zayde arguing about?" I ask. It feels almost strange to call him grandpa. I only met him once, when he, Bubbe, and Henry's sister visited us one fall when I was really young. I barely remember anything besides the great wooden hut we built outside.

Both my grandparents on his side have since passed, and I never got to know them.

Henry's face grows clouded. "It's nothing for you to worry about." He hands me back the watch. "Now that you know a little bit about it, why don't you try again?"

I cradle the watch in my hands, thinking about the story Henry told. I imagine the watch on my faceless Zayde's wrist, and then again on Henry's, the way it must have felt before the leather wore down, how light it must have been sailing through the air when he threw it. With those thoughts trapped firmly in my mind, I build my bridge again.

This time I feel it take hold.

The link between me and the watch latches into place, my

excitement swelling as the watch's story pours into my head. I see an unfamiliar man who resembles Henry in his dark brows and solemn expression. He's dressed in a soldier's uniform, his curly brown hair tucked beneath a broad cap. He hands the watch to a grim-faced woman clearly holding back tears.

The watch spends a lot of time tucked away after that, until the day the man comes back to wear it again. I spiral through its life on his wrist, jumping from important moment to important moment, until I see the one Henry told me about: when Zayde gave him the watch on his wedding day. I feel its fear of being thrown through the air, and the disorienting pain of striking the wall, but I also feel the love and affection that went into its repair.

Gradually, I slip out of the watch's memories, the distant *tick tick* of its gears pulling me back to reality.

"It worked," I say with a grin.

Henry's smile matches mine. "It makes sense. Stories bring people together. Why not objects too?"

His excitement warms me to my toes. I do a little quick math and ask, "Zayde fought in World War Two?"

"Briefly, but yes." Henry takes the watch back and slips it around his wrist. "He was part of the American forces that helped liberate the concentration camps."

I shiver, secretly glad the watch hadn't been with him during that time. I learned about the Holocaust in my homeschooling, but it has always felt worlds away when I'm surrounded by psychics and witches and a sentient house. There's also a part of me that has never really felt Jewish. Sure, we celebrate Hanukkah, and I know Henry grew up attending Hebrew school and going to temple, but he never really talks about it.

I tell people I'm Jewish, but I've never really thought about what that means.

"Tonight's the second night of Hanukkah," I prompt him, and he makes a small sound of acknowledgment, but nothing more. And just like that, we're back to awkward silence, the distance between us suddenly gaping, and I wonder if I said something wrong.

I spend the next hour practicing with other objects. My shoe, my pack, things I know the history of and can focus on to build a bridge. It's a lot easier with things I know well, but I won't be familiar with the Myrtle Staff. If I can't use my psychometry on it, we'll never find the Tree of Life, and Ashmedai will come after us for the staff.

I shiver at the thought of what will happen if Ashmedai siphons the Tree's power. The Otherworld will fall apart, magic will disappear . . . and it'll be my fault. I wanted to come, I wanted to help. I can't fail.

Colin plops down beside me and begins filling a bowl with soup. I get one whiff of sweat and push him aside. "Go stink up your own bag!"

He sniffs under his arm, makes a face, and mercifully moves to the other side of the fire. Max scurries up onto his shoulders as Salem joins us too.

"I'd say we're about a half day's walk from the Gemstone Forest," he says, ladling soup into a bowl. "Once we're there, we'll follow the river to the mouth of the Crypt."

Henry marks his page, closing his book. "I don't suppose there's any way to prepare for what kind of trials we'll find there?"

Salem shakes his head grimly. "My journal doesn't have that kind of information."

"Then I advise that we all get a good night's sleep," Henry says. "We're going to need it."

Ravenfall

It's been a long time since the house was so quiet.

It is used to the dip in activity come winter. Most people come to visit it in the fall for Samhain, when they track mud inside from the bonfires and spill their drinks with every turn of a dance, never bothering to clean up after themselves. But usually once the guests have gone, the family is still there.

Now, even they have left, and all that remains are a bookworm and a pyromaniac.

Elaine and Roy are in the kitchen arguing, as they're always arguing, and the house is trying to drown them out with thoughts of the snow settling on its eaves and the way the crackle of the fireplace reverberates in the library. Safe, contained, and nothing like those unruly sparks that leap from Roy's fingertips. A pair of guests lounge across the couches, drinking hot spiced rum and eating the maple sugar cookies the house made that morning in the shape of menorahs and dreidels.

It would be peaceful, if not for the arguing.

Against its better judgment, the house turns its attention to the siblings, who have been struggling to do the basic tasks Nora completes with ease. All they have to do are a few psychic readings, greet guests and give them directions, and tend to the grounds. The house does the rest. It cleans rooms and changes sheets, delivers baggage and heats the halls, even the one with the leaky window Roy has yet to fix.

Yet Elaine and Roy are as frazzled as the baby wyverns nesting next to its chimney.

"I'm telling you, something is wrong with the house." Elaine leans over the kitchen island with a cup of coffee in one hand and a book on Jewish mythology in the other. "Its aura is different."

The house takes offense to that. Maybe there's something wrong with *her*. She is, after all, wearing a vest over a sweater!

"Anna was saying the same thing before they left." Roy scratches his beard. He's sitting on a stool on the other side of the island, halfway through a chicken pot pie the house intended to serve the guests for dinner. "Maybe we should call Nora?"

Elaine shakes her head vigorously. "No, she's finally getting the break she needs. You were right—Ravenfall was supposed to be my responsibility once. We'll handle this ourselves."

Roy looks doubtful but takes a big bite of pie instead of responding. The house tries to scoot the pie away from him but only ends up dumping it in his lap.

Roy yelps and scurries backward off the stool, glaring at the nearest wall. "What was that for?"

The house sighs, its architecture settling with a groan. They always address it like they expect it to speak back to them. Sometimes it wishes it could. Maybe then it could tell Kara to get rid of those terrible electronics in her room, and it could make Roy keep his neat and tidy, instead of the sprawling mess it always is.

It wishes Anna were here.

Anna always knows what it wants and how to make it feel better. She'd tell Roy exactly what's wrong, starting with that ridiculous creature growing on his face! At least Henry's beard is neatly trimmed; Roy might as well go live with the gnomes down in the Faerie Garden.

It even misses Max, who changed its hat to a kippah before he left but didn't stay for his usual afternoon nap atop the chimney. He'd seemed eager to get back to the others, and who was the house to stop him. It's not like it *wanted* to spend time with the silly creature.

Most of all, the house wishes it could take a short, quiet nap. Just a quick little break to recharge, that's all it needs. After that, it won't burn breakfast anymore, or forget to close the windows at night. It won't send baggage to the wrong rooms or neglect to unlock the door when a guest loses their key.

Just a little nap, and then maybe it could shake this feeling that something is very, very wrong.

CHAPTER 8

Colin

A hand shaking my shoulder wakes me up from restless dreams of spirit-like faces, all calling my name. I blink groggily until Salem's face resolves above me. It's still dark out, though the sky is beginning to lighten. If Salem's waking me . . . I sit up abruptly, summoning my Saint Knives.

"What's wrong?" I ask, but Salem shakes his head and presses a finger to his lips, the moonlight glinting off his rings. The voices from my dreams linger. I try to force them away, but their presence persists, as if just waiting for me to turn and look.

"I'm not sure yet," Salem says quietly. "I caught the trail of something nearby. Are you up for a hunt?"

It takes me a moment to realize what he's saying: he wants to take me on a real Raven hunt, just like he promised.

Grinning, I summon away my knives and shuffle out of the warmth of my sleeping bag. Salem waits while I get dressed and lace up my boots, and then we set out without waking the others. Our breath fogs in the cool morning air, and a light mist hovers just off the ground, winding between the trees in ribbons too thick to be completely natural.

"What are we hunting?" I flex my fingers at my sides to work out my growing anticipation.

"A púca," Salem replies. "We saw it yesterday."

I think of the silver-eyed crow that transformed into a hare before disappearing in a puff of smoke. Púcas are usually harmless but can be dangerous to travelers. What I've read says they tend to take the form of a horse, enticing travelers onto their backs, before taking off on a chaotic ride. They drop their riders back where they started: dead or alive.

"It followed us?" I ask.

He nods. "It tried to get into our camp, but my wards drove it off."

A shiver that has nothing to do with the cold drops down my spine. "Do you think it has anything to do with Ashmedai?"

Salem gives me a sly smile. "Smart. I was thinking the same thing."

I straighten beneath his praise, trying to look like I expected to be right. It's not that I don't trust myself, but with Liam's attitude lately, I've started to doubt that I know as much as I think I do.

You trained for this, I remind myself. *Liam doesn't know what he's talking about.*

There's a shift in the air, and then a voice whispers, *"Oh, little Raven. Come to kill us dead?"*

I resist acknowledging the redcap's voice. It had talked incessantly as I'd tried to fall asleep last night, its rancid words following me into my dreams, and no amount of Gran's tea had done anything to help my annoyance.

The redcap makes a mocking *tsk*ing noise. *"Are you sure you can?"*

My head snaps toward the voice on reflex, and I nearly stop cold. A shimmering form occupies the space to my left, vaguely resembling the outline of the redcap.

The creature lets out a low laugh. *"You can see me now, can't you? I wonder what that means?"*

I know what it means—Fin's magic is getting stronger. I've been trying to focus on suppressing it, refusing to reach into the well of power inside me, but it feels more potent than it did yesterday, and now I can see the redcap. What if Elaine's right, and I lose control?

No, I think. *I can do this.*

I squeeze my eyes shut briefly, focusing on pulling away from the magic.

"Colin?"

My eyes snap open. Salem is a few steps ahead of me, his brow furrowed. I quickly catch up, thankful that the redcap is nowhere to be seen.

"Sorry," I say. "I thought I heard something."

"It's good to stay on alert," Salem replies encouragingly. "But let me know next time, so we can both be prepared."

I nod, relieved that he believes me. Salem doesn't know about my abilities from Fin, and I don't know what he'd think of them if he did. Probably the same thing that I do: that they make me a little *too* much like the creatures we're hunting.

He can't find out.

Salem leads me along a narrow path between two oaks, where a line of bushes obscures a clearing beyond. I can just make out the fluttering branches of another frosted willow tree, and the crow sleeping within them. It's quiet, so silent the cold feels like its own presence.

I hesitate at the perimeter. "It's just sleeping."

"And?" Salem prompts.

"Well . . . it hasn't done anything yet, has it?" I ask uncertainly. "We don't really know if it works for Ashmedai."

A look of understanding settles across Salem's face, and he sets a hand on my shoulder. "Don't you see, Colin? The Otherworld is the source of all the creatures that you hunt in the human world. If they didn't cross over to our realm, you wouldn't need to protect anyone. We can stop them here and now before it's too late to save lives."

My nails dig into my palms as I think about my parents. It's because of me that Liam and I weren't there to help them when Fin Varra and his wraiths attacked. I'd convinced Liam to do an odd job with me to help bring in some cash, and we'd returned to our motel room to find our parents already dead.

I'd been so useless that day.

If I'd known what I was, if my parents had told me the truth and trained me, I could have protected them.

Salem grips my shoulder a little tighter. "Henry told me about what happened to your parents," he says solemnly. "Something very similar happened to mine."

I blink up at him, not sure what to say. When I lost my parents, it crushed me. I still feel the weight of it, and some days I think I always will. If it weren't for Anna and the Ballinkays, I don't know what I would have done.

Salem smiles sadly and lets his hand fall back to his side. "My father was a Raven, but he didn't want to be. He refused to train me, so I started doing it myself. One night when I was out, two vampires attacked my town. My parents were among the casualties."

I swallow hard, knowing exactly what the pain in his eyes feels like. "I'm sorry, Salem."

He lifts a hand, summoning his iron blade. "It's not your fault; it's theirs." He nods at the púca, his face set in a grim line. "I made a vow that day that I would do whatever I could to ensure no one else suffered the same fate I did. Now, you don't have to get involved in that—"

"I want to," I say, my resolve growing. "I want to make the same promise. To make sure no one else gets hurt like my parents did."

The look in Salem's eyes is nothing short of proud, and it makes me feel ten inches taller. It's the look I always want Liam to give me, instead of the frown and furrow of his brows that means he's disappointed again.

"All right," Salem says. "Let's go."

We slip into the clearing, where the crow sleeps with its beak tucked under one wing. Instead of my Saint Knives, I summon an iron blade, since iron is a particular weakness of púcas.

The blade is small and thin, and I shift it so I'm ready to throw. Salem notices and gives me a little space, nodding at the tree.

He's going to let me do it.

I study the bird, my stomach squirming in a way it hasn't on past hunts. It still feels wrong to attack a sleeping creature in its own home, but Salem said it tried to get into our camp. If it weren't for the wards, it might have spelled one of us onto its back, and I doubt we would have survived the ride. And that's nothing to say of what might happen if it got into the human world, the people it could hurt.

Then there's the look of expectation in Salem's eye. I have to prove that he was right to offer to train me.

Taking a deep breath, I prepare to throw the knife—just as something bursts through the bushes behind us.

Salem and I whirl, but it's only Max, his green eyes wide and his chest heaving as if he sprinted the whole way here. It's enough to wake the púca, who spreads its wings with a loud caw and takes off into the lightening sky.

"Max," I groan. "You scared it away!"

Max clambers up onto my shoulders, peering at Salem with one narrowed eye. If the other Raven notices the scrutiny, he doesn't comment, only dismisses his blade away with a sigh.

"We'll have to keep an eye out for it while we travel," Salem says. "It may come after us now."

I shoot Max a dark look but follow Salem back to camp in

silence. This was my chance to show him I was capable of everything he thought I was, and Max had to go and ruin it because he can't be alone for five seconds.

When we get back to camp, the morning is in full effect; Henry is making breakfast and Anna is sketching birds in the dirt with a stick.

"More training?" Henry asks absently.

"We need to stay sharp here," Salem replies as we join them by the crackling fire.

Anna gives me a sideways look. "Are you okay?"

"Why wouldn't I be?" I ask, my frustration slipping.

She rolls her eyes. "I don't know, that's why I'm asking."

Rather than say something else I might regret, I shuffle over to help Henry fill plates with eggs and potatoes and slices of leftover challah. I'd never tried the thick, chewy bread before I met the Ballinkays, but it's incredibly good, with a rich buttery flavor. Max steals a potato from everyone's plate except Salem's—from his he takes two, likely penance for stepping on his tail all those years ago.

I wonder if Max ever helped Salem on his Raven missions like he helps me. Ravens have a unique connection with Jabberwockies, even when we're not bonded to them. I can feel Max's magic the same way I feel the Otherworld's magic around me, and I bet Salem can too.

We finish breakfast and pack up, Anna muttering to herself about the evils of walking as we set off through the trees. I keep my gaze moving, worried the púca might return, but nothing bothers us for the next couple hours, not even the redcap's spirit.

Gradually, a light floral scent like honeysuckle enters the air. The ground slopes up ahead into a low hill, and when we reach the top, the valley below takes my breath away. In every direction as far as we can see stretches a forest exactly like the one at our backs—except every single tree is made of gemstones.

Sprawling emerald oaks meld into ruby willows; topaz birches tower alongside big-leafed onyx maples. The ground is littered with leaves in a kaleidoscope of colors like the Tzavua's coat, the trees' branches undulating in the breeze with the flexibility of real ones. Grass reaches up between the fallen leaves and patches of snow, the trunks coated in bright green moss and crawling vines, the space between trees packed with bushes.

"This is so cool," Anna breathes, and something about it bothers me. I realize what it is when she starts down the hill without hesitation. Anna always looks at things like this and sees the magic in them, never the danger. She doesn't stop to think what those trees can do, or what might be waiting behind their trunks.

Meanwhile, all I can think of is that púca.

We descend into the Gemstone Forest. The leaves actually *crunch* underfoot like normal ones, breaking apart into flecks of gem, and they jingle in the wind like chimes. Max leaps off and begins bounding through them, knocking them into the air and crunching as many as possible.

"This feels so weird."

I spin at the sound of Anna's voice to find her with her palm flat against the jade trunk of a tree. Her eyes light up, and she holds her hand out to me. "Colin, check this out."

I swallow the urge to tell her to stop touching it and walk toward her. She grabs my hand and pulls—*hard.* Harder than she should be able to, enough to nearly lift me off my feet. I tumble into her, but she catches me with one arm and a loud laugh, steadying me.

"How . . . how did you do that?" I ask.

"The tree is full of magic," she says. "I think it made me stronger."

Henry adjusts his glasses, inspecting the trees with renewed interest. "Gemstones are extremely powerful occult symbols in Jewish mythology, among many others," he says. "They each have a particular meaning or power. Emerald is said to enhance strength and courage."

"We should all be careful." With a frown, Salem eyes Max, who is still frolicking among the leaves. "This area of the Otherworld is not well documented."

As if he hadn't heard him at all, Henry touches a sapphire tree and then blinks, removing his glasses. "Oh my. Sapphire is said to have medicinal value, in particular for the eyes."

He runs through several more gemstones as we go about touching different trees, much to Salem's dismay. Onyx brings good favor for whoever wears it. Agate keeps a person stable on foot or horseback. Amethyst is an amulet against evil spirits—that one captures my attention.

Thinking of the redcap, I pluck free an amethyst leaf and tuck it into my pocket. Almost immediately, the press of spiritual energy fades, as does the presence of the sliver of Fin's power inside me. I breathe out in relief. Maybe with this, I can keep his magic contained.

"Ow!"

Salem and I whirl as one. Anna's looking between a thin cut on the back of her forearm and the auburn jacinth tree above her.

"It just *threw* a leaf at me," she says. "And it was sharp!"

Another leaf flies out of the jacinth tree, and Anna leaps aside. It burrows into the ground like an arrow. Max snarls at the tree and herds Anna away from it.

"This is exactly what I warned you all about." Salem summons a pair of throwing knives. "Henry, Anna, get between us."

They obey, and Salem and I face outward, my Saint Knives appearing in my hands. The jacinth tree rustles and goes still.

Then an onyx oak sends a flurry of leaves straight for us.

I swipe them from the air with my knives, diverting them left and right. Salem throws a blade at the trunk of the tree, but it clatters off harmlessly. A high-pitched cackle echoes from above, and the tree attacks again.

I fend off the leaves, backing up to tighten our circle, and nearly trip over Anna, who has crouched down. At first, I think she's hiding, which seems odd, but then I realize she's trying to get a better view of the tree.

"There's something in the branches," she says. "It looks like a person, but like if a person was also a bat. Oh, it didn't like that."

Salem swings around, deflecting the latest attack. Henry

crouches beside Anna to follow her line of sight. "Oh, it's a mazzik!"

"Why is everyone in your family always so excited to see things that want to kill us?" I groan.

"I doubt it wants to do that," Henry says matter-of-factly. "Mazzikim typically cause minor chaos."

"I would not call a blade to the throat a minor chaos," Salem says grimly. "Max, defend Anna and Henry."

It's the first time he's spoken to the cat, and to my surprise, Max listens. He shifts into his Jabberwocky form, curling his long leathery body around Anna and Henry. When the next burst of leaves fly, he turns translucent, and the leaves dissolve into silver magic when they touch him. Maybe they have worked together before after all.

Salem and I take the opening to rush the tree. I spot the mazzik just as Salem sends his knives flying at it. The creature disperses and reappears on another branch, cackling. I aim for it with a knife, but it dodges easily again, rematerializing on a low branch.

It sticks its tongue out at us, its dark eyes delighted—before a look of utter disgust fills its face. With a shrill cry, it vanishes in a puff of black smoke and doesn't return.

I summon back my Saint Knife and turn to find Anna with a stick in her hand. She's cleared away a patch of gemstone leaves to reveal the dirt underneath and drawn a hamsa—a ward against evil.

She hefts the stick over her shoulder and smirks. "Not everything has to be solved with knives, you know."

CHAPTER 9

Anna

I expect Colin to be impressed with my quick thinking, but he only looks gloomier. Then again, he always looks a little gloomy, except for lately it's gloom overload with a dash of constant irritability.

I fall back beside Henry as we trudge through the Gemstone Forest, more alert than when we entered. Salem said it shouldn't take us long to reach the Pishon River, which we'll follow east toward the Crypt, but until we're inside I can't help feeling too out in the open. Between the Tzavua and the mazzik, I'm starting to see what made Fin want to escape this place so desperately.

You never know when something is going to attack.

Meanwhile, Henry reads as he walks. I peer over to see a picture of a mazzik alongside a description.

"Jewish mythology?" I ask.

He nods, clearly absorbed in the book, and disappointment

crowds my chest. I might as well try conversing with one of the trees. At least they might actually listen. I just want to spend time with him, to talk with him. I thought coming on this mission would help, and it did, for a little bit. But now it's just like it is back at home: him absorbed in a book, and me left by myself.

He never talks to us. Kara's words come back to me again, and this time, I can't ignore them. What if she's right? What if Henry *doesn't* want to talk to us?

Except a moment later, Henry says, "Did you know that Jews refer to the Otherworld as Sheol? It is said to be the place where every spirit goes after death, whether righteous or not. It is described as a land of gloom and darkness."

"Sheol," I repeat, trying out the word. I like the sound of it, but I like this conversation even more, and I latch on to it. "Does that mean they were wrong? Even the normal forest back there was pretty bright."

"Not necessarily. In fact, I think Sheol is a different place for the living and the dead, and like many things, it contradicts itself. But there's a lot to be learned by a contradiction. It forces you to really think and try to understand something."

Like how Colin can be both my best friend, and really, really annoying. No sooner do I think it than a wave of guilt hits me. Colin *is* my best friend, and instead of asking why he's been so upset lately, I've just gotten grumpy right back at him.

So much for trying to understand.

I fiddle with the strap of my pack. "I'm not very good at contradictions."

"It's not about being good at them," Henry says brightly. "It's about engaging with them. Forcing yourself to truly consider something, rather than simply draw conclusions. Like your psychometry requires you to understand an object before you can read it, instead of just presenting you with answers."

"Engage with them . . ." I glance ahead to where Colin trails a step behind Salem, idly flipping one Saint Knife back and forth in his hands. He's gotten so good at handling them, you'd never know he only learned he was a Raven a couple months ago. It's like he was born for this, though sometimes I don't think he sees himself that way.

Another contradiction: he was born with his powers, and yet has never felt enough like a Raven.

It reminds me of being Jewish.

"Do you think—" I cut off at the sound of Henry murmuring to himself. He's back to reading and taking notes, which means I've lost him, but there's something else I need to do anyway.

Leaving him to his book, I hurry on ahead. "Colin?" I call.

He slows, waiting until I catch up. "What?" he asks, knocking Max's tail out of his face. Max promptly sticks it back under his nose.

I get straight to the point. "Are you okay?"

For a moment, he looks annoyed, but then it melts into a hesitant smile. He always did say he liked my bluntness. "Sorry, I know I've been kind of grouchy."

"Like Max-without-dinner-level grouchy," I say. Max sticks his tongue out at me, and Colin laughs.

"It's not you I'm mad at," he says, and I only realize I'd been worried about that when hearing it makes me breathe easier. "It's Liam. He's been treating me like a little kid every time he's back, like I can't do anything. It's like he doesn't even remember what I did on Samhain."

That sounds familiar. Nora did the same thing to me about working at Ravenfall. Instead of using my psychometry powers, I spent all my time sweeping up faerie dust and replacing glamour pouches. Except it turned out that she hadn't realized how I felt, how much I wanted to be a part of the inn, until I told her.

"Have you tried talking to him about it?" I ask. "I bet he doesn't realize how he's making you feel."

Colin fiddles with his necklace. "I yelled at him. Does that count?"

I grin. "I don't think so."

"It won't work." We both look up to find Salem watching us over his shoulder. "His brother won't acknowledge what he's capable of until Colin shows him."

"You don't even know Liam," I reply. "He—"

Salem cuts over me. "I've met plenty of people just like him. I know their type, and I know how to handle them. Trust me, Colin. See this mission through and your brother will realize how unfair he's been."

Just like that, Colin's expression shutters, his all-encompassing frown taking over his face. "He's right, Anna," he says through gritted teeth. "Liam's not going to listen to me until I give him a reason to."

I start to argue, but he jogs to catch up with Salem, and I shut my mouth with a glower at them both.

It takes another half hour of walking through the Gemstone Forest before we hear the rush of a nearby river. We follow a sloping hill down until we find it. The waters are a silvery blue unlike any color I've ever seen, and I long to capture it in a sketch, but the true magic is in the humming.

It sounds like singing.

"Do you think it's dangerous?" Colin asks as we walk alongside it.

I think of the pond we passed earlier. Those waters were singing, too, but where that was a haunting melody, there's something joyful about this one. The water even shifts in rhythm with the sound, as if it's dancing.

"I wouldn't touch it," Salem advises. "We don't want a repeat of the trees."

I swallow back a response—that had been a mazzik, not the trees. Max locks gazes with me and rolls his eyes.

"This must be the Pishon, one of the four primordial rivers," Henry mutters in awe, scribbling something down in his book. "It is said to encircle the whole of the land."

We walk alongside it until the trees begin to thin and we near a large grassy hill. The ground slopes up toward an opening in the hill face, a single tree made of jasper standing guard. It looks like I'd imagine a tree struck by lightning would, the jasper the red brown of desert clay and the limbs thrown out in all directions.

"This must be the entrance to the Crypt." Salem slows as we near the tree. "The trials probably begin—"

"Now," says a smooth voice.

We all look around, but there's no one there.

"Up here."

We look up, but the only thing there is the tree. It shifts its branches in greeting. "Yes, hello. That was me."

Max perks up on Colin's shoulder, looking as though he might try to bat at the tree's twitching branches. The rest of us just stare.

The tree makes a creaking sound that resembles a sigh. "Always the look of surprise. Why is it that humans in a magical land are always surprised to find magic?"

Henry recovers first and steps forward. "Good afternoon," he greets the tree. "We're seeking the place where Ravens keep powerful magical objects."

"I never would have guessed," the tree replies. "To enter, you must first solve my riddle."

I groan, but Henry and Colin actually seem excited. Salem just looks annoyed.

The tree clears an invisible throat. "In four, there are seven. In seven, there are four. What was, will be, and what will be, always was."

We all wait, expecting more, but the tree goes silent. I spin the words around in my mind and come up empty.

"In four, there are seven," Henry mutters, scratching at his beard.

"A month?" Colin suggests. "It has four weeks with seven days."

"And the second part?" Salem counters.

"Months repeat every year." Colin shrugs, clearly not sold by his own argument.

"Four is a very powerful number in many belief systems." Henry begins pacing along the base of the tree. "In Jewish thought, four is a representation of seven."

I cross my arms. "What does that mean?"

Henry crouches down, using a nearby stone to draw a menorah. He does one big arcing line, then another above it, and a third above it. Then he draws a single line down the middle, resulting in seven branches, the places where the candles would go.

"There are seven candle spots, right?" Henry doesn't wait for anyone to reply before continuing. "No matter which side you count inward from, you hit the middle spot at number four. This is the source branch, whose candle lights all the others."

He points at the two outside branches on either side of the source branch. "Furthermore, each branch has a reflection on the other side, meaning there are only four unique branches instead of seven. If you follow the tip of one branch down and around"—he does just that, tracing his finger down the first branch to the bottom of the menorah, and then up again to the tip of the seventh branch—"they are connected."

I nod. "Then four and seven are the same."

"Exactly." Henry stands, dusting dirt off his hands. "Both numbers are also known to suggest completeness."

Colin's face scrunches up in thought. "So, whatever the answer is, there's either four of them or seven, and they're . . . complete?"

I nod absently, thinking of the second part of the riddle: *what was, will be, and what will be, always was.*

"Maybe *complete* is another way of saying unending?" I crouch down by Henry's drawing, tracing the outer branch. It connects one end to the other, and if you keep going—

"A circle!" I realize aloud.

Henry's earlier mutterings come back to me then: *The Pishon River is said to encircle the whole of the land.*

"The river!" I say. It's one of *four* primordial rivers that flow in a circle around the Otherworld; another representation of completeness, just like the numbers four and seven from the riddle.

Without waiting to hear the others' opinions, I dart over to the edge of the Pishon and cup my hands, collecting a little water. It's nearly all slipped through my fingers by the time I return, but I deliver the last few drops to the tree's roots.

A light silver glow creeps up the tree's trunk, and it stretches, growing just a little taller. Its branches shake and settle in a relieved sigh.

"Correct!" it says. "You may enter."

And then like a glamour falling away, the hillside *changes.*

CHAPTER 10

Anna

What was once a small opening in the hillside transforms entirely. The hill triples in height, becoming a sheer cliff face run through with jagged lines of different gemstones. The opening shifts into a massive two-paneled oak door with intricate carvings of mythological beasts accented in gold. I recognize the Tzavua roaring alongside a stag-like creature with a bird's wings, both nearly wrapped in the long tail of a Jabberwocky.

Before the doors is a thick stone staircase, each step carved with words in a hundred different languages. The cracks between the stone tiles glow with the bright silver of magic, as if the river's light fed them.

"Whoa," I say.

"Well done, Anna," Henry says excitedly, already halfway past the tree, and I grin after him. Looks like I can be useful on an expedition after all.

Salem swiftly catches up to him. "Let me go in first. We don't know what we're going to find inside."

Henry looks disappointed but agrees, and we all fall in behind Salem as we climb the stairs. Quiet whispers exhale from the steps in a hundred different languages as we go, voices too faint to make out. It doesn't stop Henry from bending down to listen, and then being herded up the rest of the stairs by Salem.

When we reach the top, the doors open of their own accord, revealing a grand cylindrical room of stone. The walls are every bit as intricate as the staircase, with golden drawings of trees and words in various languages. They feel . . . alive. Seeing as I live in a sentient inn, that shouldn't bother me, but there's something about the presence that feels watchful.

Like they're waiting to see what we'll do.

Numerous hallways sprout off from the main room, and in the very center sits a pedestal made of jacinth.

There doesn't appear to be anyone inside, so we all follow Salem in.

"There must be some way of determining which tunnel we're meant to take," Henry says. His face is nearly right up against the wall, inspecting one of the gold etched languages. When he presses a finger to it, the voices rise like on the staircase, and he makes a quick note in his journal while straining to listen. "The Crypt was built to protect powerful items but be accessible to those who knew where to look."

"My father always said only the worthy could find it." Salem surveys the towering room with a look of scrutiny. Then he toes the jacinth pedestal with his boot. "There's meant to be a logbook here of everything contained inside. It appears to have been removed."

Something about that itches at me. This is a Raven stronghold; why would a Raven have removed the logbook? I glance at the nearest wall, feeling as though it's trying to tell me something.

Colin points at the pedestal. "Elaine says jacinth can be used for scrying. I wonder if Anna can use her powers on it to see where the Myrtle Staff is located."

My stomach does a small flip as they all turn toward me expectantly. "Right," I say, fiddling with the straps of my pack and trying not to panic. I approach the pedestal and crouch beside it. It's a solid block of stone, but there's a piece in the middle that seems to have been broken off.

I know the moment I touch it that it's too distant, too unfamiliar to build my bridge. Anxiety bubbles up in my chest. We made it all the way here, and I don't want to let everyone down now that we're so close.

I don't want to let Henry down.

"Is there anything you can tell me about this?" I ask Salem hopefully.

He summons his Raven journal, flipping through the pages. "The only information I have says there will be a series of trials to reach an object in the Crypt, and to follow the directions of the logbook, which is clearly not an option."

Henry kneels beside me, inspecting the pedestal with a closer eye. "From the shape of the empty space, I suspect a column once rose up from the center. If the logbook was kept here, there was probably some sort of table at the top. Think of the people who would have leafed through its pages for information."

Gratitude sweeps through me, and I close my eyes again. This time, I focus on the details Henry gave me. I imagine a column rising up from the pedestal and ending in a small top, upon which sits a big book. As I reach out with my magic, it latches on to the pedestal, and the image in my mind changes.

Just like Henry said, the pedestal once held a small tabletop with a book, in which people recorded the items they brought to the Crypt. Time passes in a whirl through the pedestal's memories, countless Ravens coming and going. I catch a glimpse of a fist-sized diamond, a leather book whose title shines with magic, a flaming sword, what looks like a glittering wooden staff—on and on through magical artifacts and people, each one disappearing down a different hall, until—

"Ow!" I pull back, pressing a hand to my head.

"What did you see?" Salem asks urgently.

"A lot of people and objects." I rub my now aching head. It'd felt like something had slammed into me. "I think the pedestal's memory got damaged when someone broke it apart."

Salem relaxes, and Colin offers me a hand up. "Did you see where the staff is?" he asks.

I point at the central passage. "I saw someone take it that way."

The swirling golden ink and imagery continue along the walls of the corridor, until we reach a towering arch-shaped door with a pattern cut into its face. It looks like the kind of maze a scientist would send mice scurrying through, except the pathway's barely wide enough to fit my pinky finger.

"It's not a true maze." Henry tilts his head in observation. "It's a single clear path."

"That we do what with?" I ask.

Colin steps closer, inspecting the opening to the path at the top of the door. A small spike sticks out beside it. Henry notices it at the same time. "The Crypt was meant to prevent these objects from falling into the wrong hands," he says. "To Ravens, that likely meant anyone who isn't human, perhaps even anyone who isn't a Raven."

Before I realize what he means, Colin presses the tip of his finger into the spike hard enough to break skin. The drop of blood descends into the pathway, coursing downward and leaving a trail of silver magic in its wake. When it reaches the bottom, it disappears into a hole in the floor.

The door pulses with light—and then clicks open.

"Smart thinking," Salem says, and Colin practically beams. We continue down a hall identical to the one behind us, only to hit another door. Except this one has a giant stone keypad, the buttons bigger than my hands.

"A code?" Colin asks. "How are we supposed to know that?"

"Maybe there's a clue in the wall's imagery," Henry suggests.

We break up to search the corridor, but we can't read most of the languages (Colin and I only know English, and between Salem and Henry we have Russian, German, Hebrew, Yiddish, and Spanish, which isn't too shabby but still leaves about five hundred more). When I press my hand to the wall, the voices rise up, but it's like trying to focus on one conversation when my whole family is in the room talking—I can't hear a single word, but I *feel* something.

The voices—they seem confused. Like they're arguing. Beneath that, I sense something else.

Something like a warning.

A shiver shoots through me, and I pull my hand away. This place was built to protect magical objects; maybe it doesn't like that we've come to take one.

"Sorry," I tell the wall. "We have to before Ashmedai does."

We end up back in front of the keypad, trying to think of hints we might have missed.

"So far, the answers have been water and blood." I tick them off on my fingers. "What do those have in common?"

"They're both liquids," Salem offers with a shrug.

Henry snaps his fingers. "Liquids specifically tied to life."

"Okay, but life isn't a number." Colin runs his hand over the keypad, searching for clues.

"No, but in the Hebrew alphabet, each letter has an assigned numerical value." Henry steps up to the door, and Colin scoots back to give him room. "The word for 'life' in Hebrew is *chaim,* spelled with the letters chet, double yud, and mem. The numbers assigned to those letters are eight, ten, ten, and forty—or to put it another way, eight, one, zero, one, zero, four zero."

I grin. "That's really cool."

Math has never been my favorite subject, but if it can double as a secret language, that might just have to change. Maybe when we're back home, Henry can teach me the other Hebrew letters and their numbers.

Henry shares my smile as he presses the first number, and the stone key recedes into the wall. Something clicks overhead, and I look up as part of the ceiling separates. Henry hits the second and third numbers as my eyes adjust to what I'm seeing: dark metal spikes ready to snap down like teeth if we enter the wrong answer.

"Henry, wait!" I shout, but he presses the final number.

One impossibly long moment stretches in which I wait for my dad to become a human pincushion, but nothing happens.

"Maybe—" I start when there's a loud click and I launch myself at Henry with a yell. In my head, I knock him out of the way and save the day, but all that actually happens is I bounce off him like a tennis ball and end up on my butt as the door slides away into the wall.

All three of them are staring at me, and I point upward at the spikes.

Henry's face slackens, and then he's on his tiptoes trying to get a better look. "I wonder what sort of mechanism they used. A spell, perhaps?"

Colin offers me a hand up. "The more time I spend with him, the more sense you make."

"Let's go," Salem says, cutting Henry's exploration short.

We enter another circular room, the walls beveled inward with small alcoves. In each recess sits a shelf, and on the shelf rests a magical artifact. I spot a pair of ruby-encrusted daggers, a chalice-like cup, and a set of dice made of what looks like yellowed bone.

Max leaps down from Colin's shoulder and begins investigating each nook and cranny of the room, while Henry turns in slow circles, taking in the room bit by bit. The walls here are covered in the same flowing gold script, all the way to the domed ceiling above, and the whispers come without any of us touching them.

"Interesting," Henry murmurs to himself. "I suspect there are many answers to the code from many languages and cultures."

Salem strides straight over to a particular alcove, where a rod shaped like a tree branch rests. The tawny surface is smooth and shiny, like petrified wood, and tiny silver veins trace throughout it.

I join him. "That looks like the drawing."

He nods and calls, "Colin?"

Colin jogs over from where he'd been inspecting the daggers, and Salem points at the staff. "I have a feeling only a Raven can remove something from the Crypt without triggering a response. Would you like to do the honors?"

Colin's face lights up, and he takes a deep breath, then reaches for the staff. No sooner does he have it in his grip than a voice rings out.

"That, my friends, belongs to me."

CHAPTER 11

Colin

We turn as one to face the entrance, where a tall olive-skinned man with curling dark hair and bright brown eyes bordering on golden stands with his hands on his hips. He wears a threadbare white and gold vestlike garment that descends to his knees over a longer shirt, the waist tied with a blood-red sash. He grins at us, flashing a set of fangs. Max lets out a low snarl beside my feet.

My first thought is vampire, but it's broad daylight outside, and he doesn't have that "living corpse" look to him. In fact, he looks like a god come to life, nearly as muscular as Salem with . . . Are those *claws* at the tips of his fingers?

Behind him are two smaller dark-haired men, one with a wicked slash across his jaw and the other with a thick jumble of teeth crowding his mouth.

"Shedim," Henry breathes.

Demons.

The walls' voices rise, speaking quickly as Anna steps up beside Henry. "Are you Ashmedai?"

"At your service." The demon performs a small bow. "I have to thank you all; a humble sheyd such as myself couldn't hope to enter a place like this on his own, let alone pluck something from a Raven-warded keep."

He holds out one claw-tipped hand. "Now, if you'd be so kind as to give me my staff."

I toss the staff to Anna, who catches it and slides behind me and Salem, dragging Henry with her. The next moment my Saint Knives are in my hands, and Salem has a sword in his.

"You're not going anywhere near that staff," Salem says.

"Oh?" Ashmedai lifts a single dark brow. Then he jerks his head to the two behind him, who rush us.

Salem meets them halfway, and they bob and weave to dodge his sword. I start toward Ashmedai, but he vanishes, reappearing behind Anna. With a cry, she swings the staff at him. He ducks, but it's enough of a distraction for me to get between them.

I slash at the sheyd's chest, driving him back. He dodges me with ease, grinning all the while as if we're playing some sort of game. With a wink, Ashmedai vanishes again.

"Colin, watch out!" Henry leaps up beside me as I whirl to find the sheyd at my back. Henry thrusts the Seal of Solomon that he's been wearing around his neck onto his pointer finger. With its power, he can control demons like Ashmedai.

He holds up his hand and says, "I command you to stop."

Ashmedai's eyes widen, his entire body going still—and then he begins to laugh, moving slowly toward us.

"Stop!" Henry commands again, but Ashmedai's golden eyes only shine brighter.

"That ring is a poor imitation of Solomon's true magic," Ashmedai snarls. "You've been tricked."

"It's a fake?" Henry mutters, studying the ring. "But then . . . the real one . . . How?"

Ashmedai makes a low *tsk*ing sound. "What a pity."

One of the sheydim battling Salem cries out, and Ashmedai's smile falters. I lunge for his throat, but he vanishes and reappears by the other battle, where Max has transformed into a Jabberwocky. He bellows at Ashmedai, who lifts a hand, a blast of fire jettisoning from his palm. Anna shouts for Max to move, but his body goes translucent, and the fire passes through.

Suddenly, the walls of the Crypt shudder, the ground rolling beneath our feet violently enough to nearly make us lose our balance. As one, the voices that have been emanating from the walls swirl to life, agitated and angry.

"They're not meant to be in here!" Salem shouts over the clamor. "The magic is reacting to them. We need to get out quickly before this place collapses."

"Get to the exit!" I tell Anna.

She grabs hold of Henry, who's watching the battle as if it's a nature documentary, and drags him toward the open door. I join Salem and Max, who resolidifies and swipes at the nearest sheyd, sending him tumbling across the floor. A lash of his tail forces

Ashmedai to teleport away, and then Salem, Max, and I are running for the door as dust shakes free from the ceiling and items rattle and topple to the floor.

We duck into the corridor, Max transforming back into a cat, and Anna hits an inset button by the door. It slides shut with a clang. I jab at a bunch of random numbers and leap out of the way as the spikes from above come snapping down. We barrel back down the hallway, closing the second door behind us as it rattles on its hinges, and then out through the entrance to the Gemstone Forest, where the jasper tree stands guard.

Night has just fallen, and the sky is the dark purple of a bruise.

"To the river!" Henry shouts. "Ashmedai has a weakness against water."

We all hurry to the Pishon, stepping into the gentle shallows around the edges. Max clambers onto my shoulders, refusing to get wet. But when we turn back to the rumbling Crypt, no one is following us. Did we trap them?

"Let's keep to the water," Salem instructs, already striking south, back the way we came. He's barely winded, whereas I'm just catching my breath and Anna is panting heavily and clutching the Myrtle Staff to her chest.

"So that is the Lord of Demons." Henry turns his hand over in the rising moonlight, looking at the brass ring that hadn't worked. If it had been real, he would have been able to command Ashmedai. "He's not quite what I imagined. Oddly polite for an evil fellow. Strangely enough, many stories present him as a wise or benevolent figure, which I suspect is related to the complex nature of demons in Jewish texts. Demons weren't always thought of as bad."

I exchange looks with Anna, who sighs. "And I thought you said contradictions were a good thing."

Henry's face brightens. "Indeed. Some scholars believe this is a result of Judaism's attempts to reconcile religion and mythology, good and bad. It's quite fascinating."

Salem doesn't look half as enthralled. "What matters is that Ashmedai is dangerous. If he gets ahold of the Tree of Life's power, it will mean disaster."

It would mean the end of all magic.

If Ashmedai succeeds, it won't matter if Liam ever accepts me as a Raven, because I won't *be* one anymore.

"Um, does anyone else feel that?" Anna asks, lifting the staff like a baseball bat. She's waded deeper into the middle of the river, and it's up past her knees now.

"Feel what?" I ask, following after her.

Henry and Salem are already waist-deep, matching looks of furrowed confusion on their faces as if unsure how they arrived there.

"It's like something's pulling me," Anna says, the water up to her waist now. Her eyes narrow, a strange sort of tug-o'-war playing out across her face, before she says suddenly, "I ate your last chocolate chip cookie and blamed it on Max."

Max looks affronted, and I gape at her, intending to ask

"Seriously?" But as the water reaches my hips, what comes out is, "I spilled tea on your new sketchbook and told you the house threw it away."

"I unplugged Kara's computer once when she was in the middle of a huge project as revenge for making me do her chores." Anna's eyes widen with every word she speaks. She can't seem to stop, and neither can I. Something inside me compels each word out even as it draws me deeper into the water.

"I chipped one of Roy's axes after he told me not to use it."

"I gave wish cider to a really annoying guest and wished for earwax."

"One time—" We're talking over each other now, and all I can think about is that we have to move before Ashmedai finds us, but the river refuses to let me. It feels like it's flowing through me, making me a part of it, like it won't let me go until I've said every bad thing I've ever done.

Henry and Salem exchange looks, and then Henry says, "I lied about knowing something about the fountain of youth so that you'd take me on the expedition with you."

"I once—" Salem snaps his teeth together, clenching his jaw so tight a muscle twitches. Whatever is happening to us must be influencing him, too, but even as noises rise in his throat, he keeps his mouth shut and tows Henry out of the river, then Anna, then me.

Only once we're free of it does the compulsion subside, and I feel like I can breathe again. Max jumps gratefully to the ground and hisses at the water, which burbles back as if to ask, *What can I say? It's my thing.*

I back away from the grassy edge, my shoes squelching. "What was that?"

Henry takes a measuring breath before he says, "I suspect the river was compelling us to admit sins, or things we feel guilty for." He crouches down beside the water but doesn't touch it. "There is a quote in Genesis that says, 'The name of the first is Pishon; it flows around the whole land of Havilah, where there is gold. The gold of that land is good; the bdellium and the onyx stone are there.' Each of those substances relate to the removal of impurities."

Anna wrings out her hair, then rounds on me. She smacks the staff into one hand like a baton. "Now, you did *what* to my sketchbook?"

I hold up my hands. "It was an accident!"

"I'm telling the house."

"Anna—"

"It's going to leave your windows open all night and move all the spiders to your room and lock you out of your bathroom and—"

"Okay, jeez! I will get you another sketchbook!"

Anna looks mollified, but only just. She plops down in the grass and begins dumping the water out of her shoes, the rest of us following suit. The evening air is crisp with a winter chill, and we take turns keeping watch while we use the trees for cover to change into dry clothes. We're far enough south now that I can barely see the top of the Crypt over the forest, a silhouette against the darkening sky.

"Quickly," Salem commands once we're all changed. "We need to get going before Ashmedai and the others escape the Crypt."

He pulls two flashlights from his bag, handing one to Henry. "Anna, can you read the staff and tell us which way to go?" he asks.

She looks to Henry as she knots her damp hair in a bun. "What can you tell me about it?"

Henry scratches his beard. "Well, it was supposedly made from the Tree of Life. I suspect it's some kind of divining rod, which are used to seek hidden knowledge. By its name, I assume it's made of myrtle. Petrified, by the look of it, which means it's fossilized, which means it's very, very old."

"Okay." Anna looks nervous but holds the staff up to eye level. Salem nods to me, and I take up a position with Henry and Anna between us while she closes her eyes, focusing on the staff.

There's a sharp intake of breath—and then she collapses.

Ravenfall

The house is worried.

Nora called. She had a vision about all the strange things going on at the inn. "Has Anna said anything about it?" she asked.

Roy had winced, probably realizing that Nora knew nothing about the Otherworld expedition. Then, like the traitor that he is, he quickly said, "Oh, it's nothing to worry about. It's just the house acting up, upset that you're gone."

He didn't tell her about the third floor disappearing for an entire day.

He didn't tell her about the guest who walked into her room only to end up in the library.

He didn't tell her about the attic ghost howling through the night and driving several guests to leave, despite Elaine spending several hours chatting with it about its love of old buttons.

The house hadn't done any of those things on purpose. It

would never jeopardize the family's business, never risk the safety of a guest, but its magic is refusing to cooperate.

When it wants to dust a perfectly prepared cup of hot chocolate with cinnamon, it gets pepper instead. When it turns on the faerie lights threaded through the garlands on the deck railing, they fritz and spark, setting alight the holiday wreathes hanging from them.

Worst of all, there's a leak! An actual leak!

It tried to direct Roy to find it, but each time it attempted to make a wall groan in the right direction, the wall behind it made a noise. Eventually Roy got so upset with it that he refused to listen to anything it said. While normally the house was quite content to ruin Roy's day, this time it wished he wouldn't walk away.

Because the house doesn't know what is happening.

It has never lost control of its magic before. Does it have something to do with everyone leaving? Or perhaps with that strange feeling deep in its wood grain, as if the Hollowthorn is calling it home. It knows it was born of the woods, but it has since become its own being, its own magic. It didn't think such a bond still existed between them that the wood could have such an impact on it.

Yet it feels the wood pulling. Feels it reaching out.

"I'm telling you, it moved." Elaine and Roy are in the kitchen again, Elaine staring over the sink at the edge of the woods. "The tree line did not used to be that close."

Roy rolls his eyes from the kitchen table, loading his plate with another three-stack of leftover cardamom pancakes with blackberry syrup that he heats with his hands. "The wood isn't moving, Elaine. You're just losing it from lack of sleep."

She whirls on him, her wild bun even messier than usual. "Oh, and why is it I'm missing out on my sleep, hmm? Because there's a ghost screaming at all hours of the night, and every time I try to summon it in a séance, my candles go out."

"It isn't me!" Roy throws up his hands. "I have better things to do than mess with your candle flames."

"Like what?" Elaine gestures at the rest of the house. "I don't see you picking up any of the slack around here. God, I finally know what Nora feels like all the time."

Roy snorts derisively, his fingertips sparking with annoyance. "At least she has the house to help her out instead of messing everything up." He tilts his head back to the ceiling. "Can you bring the third floor back? I left one of my favorite axes in the hall closet."

The house sends a rumble in response, but it's weaker than it expects, more of a tremble, or a burp.

The house does not like burps.

Elaine presses a hand to her head and clutches her tea close. "Do you think they're okay out there?"

"With two Ravens in their party?" Roy asks. "They're fine."

The house is not so sure.

CHAPTER 12

Anna

I've never felt so much magic before.

Connecting with the staff is easier than anything I've reached out to before it, as if it *wants* to tell its story. One moment I'm standing in the shallows of the Pishon River; the next I have a bird's-eye view of a tree so incredibly gigantic, I can't see the top of it.

Roots bigger than Ravenfall snake between four massive rivers, the canopy of the tree casting a world-sized shadow across the land. Beneath its branches are impossible things, from a blanket of stars so thick it's like a photo from outer space to countless full moons interspersed with the unblinking eyes of a cat.

I see far-off destinations across the world: the rolling green hills of Ireland, a busy train station in Tokyo, the snow-dusted peaks of the French Alps. Somehow when I look at them, I know exactly where they are. I smell the petrichor, the city, the snow.

Fruits of every color and kind gather among the leaves, and I hear the call of a hundred different kinds of birds flitting from branch to branch.

Everything about the Tree of Life is at once impossible for me to understand, and yet makes more sense to me than anything I've known before.

The glimpse feels like an instant, but when I blink myself back awake, I'm lying in my sleeping bag beside a fire, a real sky of stars above me. My head aches, and I roll onto my side to find Henry studying the fake Seal of Solomon by the firelight with a furrowed brow.

"What happened?" I ask, though it comes out as more of a groan. I reach for the mug of Gran's tea someone set beside me, now cold, and drink it all. It's cardamom rose, to ward off inner chills and frights. The same tea Gran first gave me and Colin after we faced down a wraith.

Henry shoots me a relieved look. "Oh, thank God, you're all right. You fainted when you tried to read the staff. You've been out an entire day. How are you feeling?"

My body aches, but I think that's from sleeping on the forest floor. I do some groggy mental math. We arrived here after the first night of Hanukkah, camped out once, and emerged from the Crypt on the third night, which makes tonight the fourth. The holiday has been helping me keep track of how long we've been gone, and it's longer than the few days we expected.

I hope Aunt Elaine and Uncle Roy aren't too worried.

Carefully, I sit up, clutching my empty mug. There's a pot over the fire bubbling with soup, and a stack of clean dishes beside it that tells me no one's eaten yet. My stomach rumbles.

"I'm okay, just hungry," I say. "How far away are we from the Crypt?"

"The only word we got out of you after you collapsed was 'north'; then you were out, so we've been traveling that direction. Thankfully you're not too big to carry yet." He smiles when I scowl. "What did you see in your vision?"

"I . . . I'm not sure how to describe it." I try my best, but it's like trying to explain something as unknown as the most distant stars. I just can't find the right words.

"It sounds fascinating," Henry says, though he adjusts his glasses in a move I've come to realize means he's nervous.

"Where are Colin and Salem?" I ask.

"Training." Henry goes back to studying the ring, holding it up to the fire's light. "After our encounter with Ashmedai, Colin is more insistent than ever to learn from him."

Something about that bothers me, but I can't figure out what. Maybe I'm still just upset that Salem acted so sure about Liam without even knowing him, or maybe it's that Colin's been obsessed with him ever since they met. I feel like I've barely talked to Colin the last couple days.

Or maybe I'm just annoyed at him for ruining my sketchbook.

"Anna, can you try reading this for me?" Henry hands me the fake ring. I take it, the brass warm from his fingers. "If it were real, it would have enabled me to command Ashmedai, but he clearly wasn't affected. I went through a lot of trouble to find that thing, though, which means someone else went through a lot more trouble to replace it with a replica before I found it."

"But why?" I turn the ring over in my hands.

Henry shrugs. "I assume so that no one would know the real one had been taken and come looking for it."

Closing my hand around the ring, I focus on a few details: it's made of brass, it has a pentagram carved into it, and it's not the real ring. Someone replaced the real one with it—yet every time I try to build my bridge, the magic refuses to latch on to it.

I try again, and again, but it's no use. I end up handing the ring back to Henry without making eye contact. "Sorry. Some things just really don't want to talk to me."

Like Colin, apparently. And my dad.

Henry frowns but doesn't say anything, and my chest tightens. So much for using magical objects to connect. First the chest wouldn't talk, ruining my welcome home present, and now the one time my dad actually asks for my help with one of his expeditions, all I do is let him down.

"I'm, uh, going to go get the others for dinner," I say, desperate to escape the growing awkward silence.

He doesn't even look up, so I scurry away as quickly as I can, following the distant sounds of wood on wood.

"Stupid object reading powers," I mutter, kicking a pebble along ahead of me. I don't know what's worse: thinking my powers are useless or knowing they're useful and not being able to harness them the way I need. Suddenly, all I want is for Nora to be here. She'd know what to do and how to make me feel better, even if it's just a warm hug.

I've never been away from her like this. I miss her.

The sounds of sparring grow louder, and I find an opening between two trees that leads into a clearing. Max sits nearby, watching Salem and Colin train with narrowed eyes. He's another one that's been acting strangely, more uptight than his normal, playful self.

You're being hunted by the Lord of Demons, I remind myself. *Even Max has his limits.*

"That isn't good enough, Colin," Salem says when Colin fails to block one of his blows. They both have a wooden training blade in one hand, and from the way Colin's wincing, I don't think it's the first time Salem's attack has gotten through. He looks one step away from collapsing, and I wonder how long they've been at this.

"I'm tryi—" Colin starts, but Salem speaks over him.

"Try harder. You're never going to protect anyone if this is the best you've got." He brandishes a hand at the trees beyond them. "These creatures? They're responsible for the deaths of your parents and mine and countless others. You have the opportunity to do something about that. Do you understand?"

Colin wipes the sweat off his brow with his sleeve. "Yes."

There's something about the way Salem's talking that makes me uneasy. It just feels . . . wrong. I want to step into the clearing and defend Colin, to say he's doing the best that he can and not to push him so hard.

Salem lifts his practice blade. When Colin comes at him,

there's a look in his eye I don't recognize at first because it looks so out of place on his face—fury.

It's the same look Fin had when he faced off with Colin outside Ravenfall.

Like he wants to destroy something.

"Dinner!" My voice rings through the clearing, bringing them both to a halt. I didn't even realize I'd stepped forward, and my heart is thudding as if I'd just called for the Tzavua's attention, instead of the boy who's supposed to be my friend.

But that look on his face . . .

Salem frowns at the interruption, but Colin's eyes brighten in his typical response to food, and I relax a little.

He's still Colin.

We return to the campfire, where I fill them in on what I told Henry about the tree over bowls of chicken and dumplings. He's still absorbed in his book, his dinner quickly growing cold.

"The staff was practically pulling me this way," I tell them. "I think it's like a magnet for the tree."

"We should be able to make good time tomorrow, then," Salem says. He hasn't touched his food, and he's tapping his fingers impatiently on his knee.

I look around the camp. "Where is the staff, anyway?"

"In my pack." Salem's tapping stills. "You dropped it when you fainted, and we nearly lost it to the river."

I wince. Of course I almost botched everything.

"We should link it to your journal," I tell Colin, who's already on his second bowl of soup and eyeing the stack of cardamom orange sugar cookies the house sent with interest. "That way if something happens to it, you can always summon it back."

"That isn't necessary," Salem says before Colin can reply. "It's safe with me."

Annoyed, I press, "It'd be even safer in the journal."

"Linking it to a journal limits our ability to access it," Salem counters with a shake of his head. "Trust me, Anna. I've been in situations like this before."

And you haven't.

He doesn't say it, but I can feel the words hanging at the end of his sentence. When neither Henry nor Colin chime in to support me, I relent, and Henry and Salem turn to review our supplies and discuss plans for tomorrow.

Meanwhile, I pull out my sketchpad and attempt a few basic sketches of the Myrtle Staff. The others prepare for bed and climb into their sleeping bags, and I pretend to do the same, waiting until Henry's soft snores fill the air before shimmying out. I check that Salem is asleep, too, before pulling the Myrtle Staff free of his pack and tiptoeing over to Colin.

I shake him awake and press a finger to my lips when he blinks groggily up at me. "What now?"

"I want to link the staff to your journal," I whisper.

He sits up, rubbing at his eyes. "Salem said—"

"I know what Salem said, but I think he's wrong. If Ashmedai escapes the Crypt, he'll be trying to find us and take the staff. If we link it to the journal, we can protect it." That, and part of me is starting not to trust Salem. Why would he be so against linking the staff?

Colin glances over at Salem's sleeping form. "Shouldn't we just wait until morning and tell Salem that?"

"And what if Ashmedai finds us tonight? Or someone else tries to take it?" I ask. "We'll tell him in the morning. You can always break the link."

Colin sighs. "If it means I can go back to sleep, fine." He summons his Raven journal and hands it to me. I fish a pencil out of my bag and start sketching. It's a simple drawing, but I take my time with the shading, getting all the veining as close as I can.

Colin lies on his back beside me, staring up at the stars while I work. Max curls up between us, and we share a mug of Gran's Earl Grey tea, which brings the drinker good dreams.

I glance at Colin, whose expression is pinched, and ask quietly, "Are you okay?"

He turns his head to look at me. "Why do you keep asking me that?"

I stare at my drawing, suddenly uncomfortable. "I don't know. It's just . . . You seem kind of different."

"Meaning?" He props himself up on one elbow. Max blinks open sleepy eyes, watching us.

"Just . . . different." I wave a hand, growing nervous. Here I go again, just saying things before I've thought them through. I want to bring up Salem, but Colin's looking at me like he's one wrong word away from mutinying, and I don't want to make him angrier, or wake up Salem. This is worse than talking to Kara! If only Rose were here, her empathy would be able to tell me what's wrong.

"Never mind, forget I said anything." I focus on my drawing, finishing the last of the shading, and hand it to him. "Here."

He takes it with a frown but lets the conversation go. Setting the staff atop the journal, he closes his eyes. A moment later the staff vanishes, and the drawing on the page takes on a lifelike quality, the veining in the branch now as bright as real silver.

We turn in after that, but I can't sleep and just end up staring at the stars. A light snowfall starts, but the flakes hit the wards and melt in puffs of silver light like falling stars. I can't shake the feeling that something is wrong. It feels like the last couple weeks at Ravenfall, with Nora packing for her trip and the twins preparing to go look at colleges. Like everything's changing and I can't make it stop.

I turn over in my bag, drawing a menorah in the dirt with my finger. I make marks for the candle flame above the source branch and the four farthest to the left, and though I don't know the Hebrew words my dad usually speaks, I stare at the menorah until the firelight dims.

Only the light of the moon and stars remain as a soft, haunting howl carries through the wind. I recognize the sound—it's a Jabberwocky.

Another voice joins the first, until they're chorusing into the night. When I roll over, I see Max in the glow of the dying firelight, his head tilted back to the sky.

CHAPTER 13

Colin

When I wake the next morning, I just want to turn over and go back to sleep. My body is exhausted from training with Salem last night, and even though I feel better now, my sleeping bag is warm and comfortable. At least I finally slept through the night without dreams of spirits. I can't even feel them now, with the amethyst gemstone tucked into my pocket to repel them, and the redcap has been quiet.

Then I smell eggs cooking, and my stomach rumbles.

Yawning, I stretch and open my eyes—and for a moment I think I'm somewhere else entirely. It was dark by the time we set up camp last night, but the clearing looks completely different in the daylight.

The bushes are a deep emerald green unlike any color I've seen and ripe with thick black berries. A massive willow tree hangs over us, its branches bright with blue and pink flowers I've never seen on that kind of tree. When the wind blows through them, they make a gentle chiming sound. The temperature is perfect, the air sweet with the scent of honeysuckle.

It's so idyllic, I want to stay there forever.

"You're awake!" Anna waves at me from the morning camp-fire, where she and Henry are cooking breakfast. Salem and Max are nowhere to be seen.

I join them by the fire. Anna holds out a handful of the dark berries from the nearby bushes and says, "You should try these. They're amazing."

Her lips are stained dark purple, Henry's too. I reach for them even as something tells me not to. Rose tells Anna about edible plants all the time; surely she'd know if these are safe? But I can't shake the feeling that there's something strange about all of this. The impossibly beautiful glade, the plump fruit, even the broad smile on Anna's face when last night all she could do was stare at me like a puzzle.

I study her more intently. There's a glazed-over look in her normally vibrant eyes. The scent of something singed fills the air, and I glance at Henry to see him flipping the same burnt piece of toast over and over again even as he eats more berries.

"Henry?" I ask. He only smiles at me, seeds stuck between his teeth.

Anna nudges me with her outstretched hand. "Try some."

I grab the berries and toss them into the fire. They hit the flames and sizzle, turning to a thick black sludge.

"Well, that was rude," says a high, feminine voice with an Irish accent.

A woman steps out of the willow tree—literally. She emerges from its trunk as if she'd been a part of it. With a simple white dress, red hair past her waist, and snake-like green eyes, she'd almost look human, if it weren't for her delicate pointed ears, nearly translucent white skin, and the impossible grace she moves with.

"You're a fae." I scramble to my feet. "This is all a glamour."

As soon as I say it, the façade of the glade falls away, replaced with the clearing I remember from last night. It looks so dull and lifeless in comparison, the colors muted and the air stale. A feeling I can't name settles hard in my chest, and I fight the urge to just sit down and give up.

A smile curls her painted lips. "Longing for my illusion? It was quite beautiful, I know."

I've read about this kind of glamour. There are stories of humans growing so attached to false worlds that when they're brought back to reality, they spiral into depression and eventually die or else spend their lives desperately trying to get back.

"Let them go," I order.

She tilts her head. "I am Saoirse of the Summer Court, and I don't take commands from humans. Not even those of Fin Varra's blood." I recoil, and her smile widens, baring a set of sharp fangs. "Oh yes, I know who you are, little Raven. Do you?"

"What? Yes, I—" I falter, not really sure how to answer her.

Saoirse laughs, a musical quality to the sound that draws me toward her before I realize what I'm doing. I dig my nails hard into my palms and force myself to stop.

"Oh, you are strong." She lifts long fingers to play with the fiery strands of her hair. "And here I thought Fin's power had whittled away to nothing. What a gift he's given you, little Raven. Why do you reject it?"

I grit my teeth against the lure of her voice. "He killed my parents. He's a monster. I don't want anything from him."

"He was a god," she says. "You are a child playing at magic."

Her words hurt more than I want to admit. She sounds like Liam, so sure that she knows me better than I do. That she has all the answers, and I should just do what I'm told. But doing what I'm told kept me in the dark about my family's legacy my entire life, and look how that ended.

Saoirse steps closer, her voice softening. "Come now, I'll make you a deal. I consider it a stroke of fate that our paths crossed, as I so rarely return here, and a power such as yours would be useful to me. If you come with me into the fae realm, I can teach you about your powers, your history, your people. I can teach you what it means to be the King of the Dead."

"I don't want to know what it means," I snap. "I don't want to know any of it."

A vicious smile cuts across her face. "You think you have a choice, boy? Fin's power is in your blood."

I flinch. I want to tell her she's wrong, but I can't. Because I can *feel* his power inside of me, coiled like a creature waiting to be woken. The amethyst helps, but what am I supposed to do, carry a gemstone with me everywhere I go and hope that it's enough to suppress his magic? What if it keeps getting stronger like Elaine warned?

"Tell me, have the voices started yet? The spirits clinging to you like thorns?" Saoirse *tsks* pityingly. "Soon you won't be able to touch someone without their life magic invading you."

I shiver at the warning in her voice. Fin's power lets me manipulate life magic, and it connects me to the Otherworld, but Elaine has long theorized that's not all it can do. What else lies in store for me if I don't get this under control?

Saoirse's grin shows too many teeth. "If you do not learn to harness your power, it will consume you. But I can teach you to control it. To suppress it if you wish."

My head jerks up, and her smile curls with satisfaction. "How do you think I found you?" she presses. "Your power calls out to us like a siren's song. I will not be the last to answer."

A shiver cuts through me at the thought of what she's describing. Fin's power taking hold of me, using it outside my control. Of the creatures that would come looking for me, like she did. The kinds of creatures I'm meant to protect people from. What if someone gets hurt because of me?

What if . . . what if *Salem* finds out?

He won't, I promise myself. I'll find a way to control my abilities myself. I'm a Raven, not the King of the Dead.

I lift my head. "I don't want anything from you, and I don't want anything of Fin's."

Saoirse bares her teeth in a hiss. "Fine, let us try another way, then. Come with me, and I'll free your friends."

Suddenly she's before me, the space between us gone though I didn't see her move. She tilts my chin up with one long finger. "If not, you can watch them waste away to dust."

I feel my mouth moving of its own accord, feel myself begin to agree even as my mind screams not to. Then something bites my ankle—hard. I yelp, pulling my leg away from Max's fangs. He gives me a look that might as well say, *Are you daft?*

Saoirse's glamour falls away, and I seize control of myself again. Summoning an iron blade, I hold it to her throat. She goes still.

"How about I make *you* a deal?" I press the tip of the blade against her skin. One prick of iron, and she'll die, like any other faerie. "Release my friends and I don't kill you."

Saoirse bares her fangs at me. "If I die, they remain stuck in that glamour."

"Which can be broken," I say, pulling from weeks of study. No glamour lasts forever. Some fade on their own, but particularly strong ones can be broken with waking herbs and spells.

She scoffs. "Before you get them out of this forest alive? I don't think so."

I tilt my knife in warning. "At least you'll be gone."

The threat strikes home, and I keep my face empty, hoping she buys my bluff. I still don't know where Salem is. Without his help, I can't get Henry and Anna out of the forest and defend us, especially with Ashmedai hunting us down, but Saoirse doesn't know that.

Saoirse hesitates, then says, "Very well. Bargain struck." With a snap of her fingers, the lingering magic in the clearing disperses.

The glazed look in Henry's and Anna's eyes vanishes, and Anna turns, throwing up a mouthful of black berries. Henry wobbles, looking ill, and Max bounds over to check on them.

"I fulfilled my end of our bargain, Raven," Saoirse snarls. "Now lower your blade."

I know I should, but all I can think about is Salem. He'd never miss the chance to rid the world of another monster. Who knows how many people Saoirse has hurt, how many lives she's taken or ruined with her glamour? If she had her way, we'd all be under her control.

These creatures? They're responsible for the deaths of your parents and mine and countless others. Salem's words from last night come back to me. *You have the opportunity to do something about that.*

A real Raven wouldn't let her go.

I grit my teeth and say, "I don't take orders from monsters."

I summon another iron knife, intending to drive it into her chest, when Anna shouts, "Colin, don't!"

I flinch, half turning as Saoirse tries to jerk away. My blade cuts a thin line beneath her jaw.

It's all it takes.

Saoirse lets out a piercing scream as the skin along the cut begins to bubble and hiss. The reaction travels along her entire body, as if she's burning from the inside out.

I want to stop it, to do something, but I can't move. My body doesn't feel like my own.

The fae gives one last, tortured scream before she collapses to the ground and her body turns to ash.

My stomach roils with a nauseous guilt. It's one of the more gruesome deaths I've seen, and it only makes my doubt worse, but I have to believe that I did the right thing. Still, I feel light-headed as I stare at her remains. Then there's a hand on my shoulder stabilizing me, and I look up into Salem's steady gaze.

"It's okay, Colin," he says. "You did the right thing."

"He *lied* to her," Anna protests, struggling to her feet. Max hovers beside her, waiting to help if she needs it. "They made a bargain!" Her face is pale, her lips still smeared purple. She looks like a corpse. She almost was one, and all she cares about is a broken deal?

Salem faces her. "He did what he had to in order to protect you and Henry. That fae would not have shown you mercy."

I latch onto his words, letting them bring me back down to earth. "All I was trying to do was keep you safe," I tell her. "She wanted to leave you in that glamour forever and let you starve!"

Anna clenches her fists, looking like she wants to say more to me, but ends up spinning on Salem instead. "And where were you this whole time?"

"Out canvasing the area for signs of Ashmedai," he replies calmly. He's always calm, ready to handle any situation that arises. I wish I could do the same, but my body feels like it's on fire half the time, I'm so angry.

For a moment, I think about holding my breath like I used

to, about forcing the emotions away, but I know that won't help. I just wish I wasn't so *mad*. Then Anna and I could actually talk without yelling at each other, and I could make her understand why I did what I did, and then maybe I'd understand myself.

I know who you are, little Raven, Saoirse's words come floating back. *Do you?*

Anna doesn't look convinced at Salem's answer, but she lets it go, instead focusing on getting the berry juice off her skin. Then she helps Henry pack up the camp and we set off in silence. After an hour or so, Anna takes the Myrtle Staff from Salem to read it again, and we adjust course a little. It's not until she hands it back to him and rejoins Henry in the lead that I remember—I linked it to my journal!

In the midst of everything with Saoirse, I completely forgot to tell Salem, and bringing it up now feels weird. What if he thinks I was trying to hide it from him? Guilt snakes through me, and I tighten my grip on my pack straps. Should I tell him or not?

Salem drops back to walk alongside me. He gives me a sympathetic look, and I wonder if my debate is plain on my face. "Don't let her get to you," he says gently, and I relax when I realize he thinks I'm still upset about Anna. He's not wrong. "She doesn't understand the responsibility you carry. You saved her life."

Then why do I feel so terrible? I want to ask, but the words won't come. Somehow, I know it would disappoint Salem to hear them, and I don't want that. All he's asked of me is to be strong, to be a real Raven.

"I only wish you'd been given the support you deserve," Salem says with a sigh. "Your brother has been holding you back. If he hadn't, you wouldn't have even hesitated back there."

I wince. "I'm sorry."

Salem studies me for a moment, his expression softening. "I've been thinking a lot about this. If you want, I can take over your training, permanently."

I stop, caught off guard. "You mean, like an apprenticeship?"

"If that's what you want," he replies. "We could even stay at Ravenfall for a while if you'd prefer, or we can set off right after this mission."

It feels almost too good to be true. After weeks of Liam dismissing me, having someone who believes in me enough to make this offer feels like flying. I almost say yes right away, but then I think about Ravenfall and my life there, about Anna and Max and all the others.

Would Liam be angry with me? Would he understand?

"Can I think about it?" I ask, worried he'll take back the offer.

Salem smiles and grips my shoulder. "Of course, take all the time you need. But remember this: You're a hero, Colin. Don't let anyone tell you otherwise."

His words settle in all the hollow places inside me, chasing away the cold. I'm a hero, not a monster. I'm not Fin, who tore through people's lives for his own selfish goals, no matter how much of his power I have, and I'm not some kid to be left on the sidelines while Liam does all the hard work.

I'm a Raven.

CHAPTER 14

Anna

That night when we make camp, while Colin and Salem are off training under Max's watchful eye, I try to work up the courage to talk to my dad about Salem. Like always, Henry's buried in a book by the fire. I don't want to bother him, but I'm also starting to get really worried.

The way Colin had looked when he'd killed that fae, how torn up he'd been until Salem told him it was all right—it made me feel like grabbing Colin's hand and running as far away with him as I could.

I know Salem is one of the good guys, that he's here to help protect the Otherworld, but I just can't stop thinking about it and I don't know what to do. Maybe Henry will.

Taking a deep breath, I go sit by Henry. It takes him a moment to notice me, and I wait until he's looking to ask, "Can I talk to you about something?"

He glances longingly down at his book, then folds it closed, his finger marking the page. "What about?"

"Colin's been acting really weird lately," I say. "And I think it's because of Salem."

Henry frowns. "Are you talking about this morning with the fae? I admit I was a little disoriented until those berries wore off, but didn't Colin save us?"

That's the thing—he *did* save us. I don't doubt for a second that our lives were in danger. But he made a deal with her, and then he broke it like it was nothing. The Colin I know is one of the most trustworthy, honest people around. So many people lied to him in his life, kept things from him, that he's never been one to do it himself.

"He's just been so grumpy lately, and I don't know why," I say.

"He's a teenager."

"*I'm* a teenager!"

Henry blinks at me as if he's only just realized that, and I groan. "I think Salem is maybe making him worse. Not on purpose, but . . ." I trail off, shrugging helplessly.

Henry sighs. "We can't pretend to know what being a Raven is like. Salem has been doing this for decades."

"But has he always been like this?" I ask. "So . . . intense?"

"For as long as I've known him, he's always been a bit gruff," he replies with a nod. "You can hardly blame him, though. He's been through a lot. He lost his parents young to a monster attack much like Colin did and has been fighting ever since."

I wince. I hadn't known that, but while it helps me understand him a little more, it doesn't make me any less worried about Colin.

"I trust that he won't steer Colin wrong." Henry flips his book back open, and I rush to respond before I lose him.

"Maybe you can tell me about him? Like about your expeditions with him?" Maybe if I know more about him, I'll feel better. But it's like Henry didn't even hear me, his attention wrapped up in the book once more.

My nails dig into my palms, my mind racing to find the words to make him listen, but that's just it: he *never* listens to me. Maybe Kara was right after all, and he just doesn't care. Is that why he spends so much time away? Part of me wants to ask, but the other part doesn't want to hear the answer.

I always thought of my dad as this great magical explorer off on quests, but I realize now that I don't know him as well as I thought I did. I imagined that if I ever went on one of his expeditions with him, it'd be full of magic and adventure and stories told over crackling fires. Now I know it's just a lot of silence and reading.

As I look at him, with his face in his book again, he feels farther away than ever.

That night, I stay awake after everyone else has gone to sleep. My talk with Henry only made me feel worse about Salem, and

I resolve to do something about it myself. Once he's asleep, I'll creep over and use my psychometry to try and read him. If there's something suspicious in his past, or if he's planning something with Colin, maybe I can find it.

Once I'm sure everyone's asleep, I start to shuffle out of my sleeping bag. I'm nearly free when Salem sits up, and I duck back down. He slips out of his bag, surveys the camp, and then disappears into the trees. Where could he possibly be going?

I wait until he's outside the wards before shoving on my boots and following him.

The woods seem thicker at night, and the trees make it hard to keep him in sight. It doesn't help that I left my sweater behind in the warmth of the wards, and the snow is thick on the ground. Surely he can't be going far? I think at first that he must be patrolling, but he's not scanning the area or going in a circle. He's heading straight for something.

My foot hits a stick, and it snaps like crackling ice. I duck behind a tree, holding my breath.

The night is silent. The kind of quiet that makes you want to glance over your shoulder, just to make sure nothing's there.

When I finally work up the courage to peek around the trunk, Salem is kneeling in a patch of moonlight, picking what looks like lavender from a bush.

I drop my head back against the tree, feeling foolish. He just came out to get herbs for tea to help him sleep. He's the only one who hasn't been drinking Gran's brews, claiming he doesn't like foreign magic in his body.

"Guess I owe him an apology," I mutter.

I peer back around the tree, intending to ask Salem to walk back with me, but he's gone.

My heart stutters, and I look around frantically, but he's no-where to be seen—and neither is camp.

"Calm down, calm down," I tell myself, trying to breathe slower. I'll just go back the way I came.

Except as I retrace my steps, nothing looks familiar. It's like the trees up and rearranged themselves while I wasn't looking, and the boot prints I surely left in the snow are gone. What little light once trickled through the canopy from the stars has faded, until I can barely see my hand in front of my face.

Something rustles in the nearby underbrush. I whirl toward it, but then another sound swishes behind me. I retreat, putting my back against a tree. No sooner do I touch it than the bark begins to creep over my shoulder like curling fingers. I leap away from it with a gasp, and the bark retreats, the tree giving an indignant shake as though it can't believe I wouldn't allow myself to be swal-lowed up.

Above, something makes a sharp chittering noise. Then a pair of glowing green eyes appear before me. I'm one second away from screaming before I realize I know those eyes.

"Max," I breathe in relief.

He winds around my ankles and then starts back the way he came, his body turning a translucent silver that lights the way.

I follow him back to camp, where I'm surprised to find Salem fast asleep in his bag.

Feeling even more foolish, I climb into my own. I can still feel the place on my shoulder where the tree tried to entomb me, and I struggle to get warm, even so close to the fire. Max clambers in after me and curls up in my arms, his warmth fighting away the chill until I finally fall asleep.

In the morning, he's gone.

I roll over, patting the spot where he was lying, but it's gone cold. I sit up, expecting to find him with Colin, but Colin is lacing up his boots and chatting with Salem while Henry prepares breakfast. A quick look around tells me he's not in camp.

"Where's Max?" I ask, joining them by the fire.

"Those Jabberwockies came by again early this morning," Salem says. "He took off after them. It's probably been a while since he's seen any others. I'm sure he'll be back soon."

I start to say that Max wouldn't have left without telling me when Salem pulls a stalk of lavender out of his mug, reminding me of how it went the last time I accused him of something. He'd just been out getting herbs, and I'd almost ended up tree food for my trouble.

Besides, Max had looked pretty forlorn listening to the Jabberwockies sing the other night. He was probably looking for them when he found me last night and went back to join them after I fell asleep.

Still, I wish he'd said goodbye. He's the only one here who doesn't feel like a stranger.

We pack up camp, and Colin hands me the Myrtle Staff. I

connect to the bridge of magic I built, but don't follow it all the way down, not wanting to be overwhelmed by the tree again. The magic feels stronger this time, pulling me in the direction we've been traveling.

I come up from the magic. "Keep going the way we are. I think we're really close. Like another day of walking."

"Let's get moving, then," Salem says. "There's no telling how close Ashmedai is to finding us."

We pick our way through the trees in silence. After a little while, Colin drops back to walk beside me. He has that look on his face that I know means he's trying to decide how to say something and can't find the words. Unlike me, who just blurts out whatever she's thinking, like, *Hey, do you think your old friend the respected Raven who took us on this selfless quest is actually a bad person?*

I cringe thinking of my conversation with Henry last night. He probably thought I sounded ridiculous, but after Salem refused to let Colin link the staff, something just felt *off.*

"I'm sorry." Colin's voice surprises me, and I look up at him. "About yesterday. I just—" He cuts off, tilting his head. "Do you hear that?"

A distant rumble rolls through the air, and the ground vibrates. Salem slows, looking troubled. The ground shakes again, more intensely this time, and I throw out my arms for balance.

"What's happening?" Henry asks, clinging to a nearby tree.

Ahead, the ground splits open with a deafening crack. Trees pour into the widening crevice as something else rises from the depths. A gigantic, horned worm easily the size of three Jabber-wockies emerges from the earth. Its skin is a pale royal purple, with three ridges of gold spikes along its body. When it opens its mouth to roar, I see circle upon circle of sharp teeth.

And standing atop its head, grinning at us all, is Ashmedai.

CHAPTER 15

Colin

"The Shamir Worm," Henry breathes in awe. He's got that same look of curiosity on his face Anna gets when she talks about something magical and dangerous.

Except this time, even Anna is backing away. "The what?" she demands.

"A creature capable of cutting through any substance," Henry explains. "Don't go anywhere near its mouth."

Anna groans. "Like I was planning on it."

"It's only supposed to be one-third of an inch," I hear Henry mumble. I've realized by now that any time we end up in a dangerous situation, he resorts to muttering about mythology. But like Max, I suspect the worm has a different form in the Otherworld as it does in ours. And if there's one thing I know, it's that mythology is one big gray area.

I summon my Saint Knives, rushing to Salem's side. He's holding a quarterstaff I've never seen him use before.

"Apologies for the delay," Ashmedai calls down to us. "I had to take a detour to retrieve a friend of mine."

Despite having traveled through the earth, his white and gold clothes are spotless, his dark hair curled as if freshly pressed. "Now, then, will you be handing over my property, or do I need to come and take it from you?" he asks with a fang-baring grin.

"You're not getting the staff!" I yell back. "And you're not getting the power of the tree."

Ashmedai chuckles darkly. "Young Raven," he teases. "How little you know."

"Enough!" Salem brandishes his quarterstaff. It's all black save a silver stripe around each tip, and I feel a strange power emanating from it.

"Indeed," Ashmedai agrees. "Your choice is made, then."

The worm wiggles and writhes, and then it opens two bright green eyes—and the tree in front of us disintegrates to ash.

"Oh, that's right," Henry mutters. "It's the eyes, not the teeth."

Anna seizes his hand and drags him behind another trunk as Salem and I rush the worm. I send a Saint Knife flying, and it buries in the worm's chest, freeing a line of green blood. I summon the blade back and throw the other, which strikes home, but the wounds are like pinpricks to the worm.

The worm flicks its tail around, and Salem and I leap aside. I tumble to the ground, letting my Saint Knives vanish so I don't cut myself. Back on my feet, I barely manage to scurry aside in time to dodge another swipe of the worm's tail. It moves quickly for its size, and when its tail slams into a nearby tree, the spikes along its edge sheer right through it.

Just like the Tzavua, I don't know what to do against a creature of this magnitude. If only Max were here, he could face it in his Jabberwocky form. Without him, I feel like a gnat buzzing at a lion, like there's nothing I can do to help, while Anna and Henry watch wide-eyed from behind a tree.

Then Salem's at my side. I expect him to tell me to hide, to leave it to him, but he only gives me an expectant look. "Even a creature this size has a weakness. Think, Colin."

I look to the worm, unable to imagine how a creature like that could possibly have a weakness. Its entire body is plated in purple scales and tipped with golden spikes from nose to tail—except for the one place I don't want to go anywhere near, of course.

"Its eyes!"

Salem's expression turns proud—and then the worm's gaze finds the ground before us. The earth turns to mud, trapping our feet like quicksand. I try to rip free, but every step digs me in deeper.

"That's enough dancing around," Ashmedai says. "The staff, if you please."

Panic lances through me, the sand already up to my waist. I hear Anna call my name, see her hand the Myrtle Staff to Henry and prepare to make a dash for me.

"Don't!" I yell, and she hesitates.

With an impossible calm, Salem drives his quarterstaff into

the earth and uses it to pry himself out. Spinning about, he holds out the end to me and I seize it, letting him drag me free. The sand goes still behind us.

Salem hefts his quarterstaff. "You can have this one instead," he calls, and leaps for the worm. He brings his quarterstaff down on the side of the worm's body, and the creature bellows in pain. Salem barely lands before he swings again as if hitting a home run. The power of the strike radiates through the worm's body.

It thrashes, and Ashmedai leaps from its head onto a nearby branch with a hiss. "Your quarterstaff is enchanted."

"To hit with three times my strength," Salem confirms. Then he leaps into the air and brings the quarterstaff down on the thrashing worm's head—right into its eyes.

The creature goes still—then its body turns to stone, and it crumbles apart bit by bit, disappearing into the crevice it emerged from.

Just like that, it's over, and I can't stop staring at Salem. He defeated such a huge opponent so easily, without ever losing his cool. The only other Raven I've ever seen hunt is Liam, but never like this. Is this what a Raven is really capable of?

What I might be capable of?

Ashmedai scowls. "Another round in your favor, Raven, but I'll be back for a third."

"Don't let him get away!" I lunge forward, and Salem sends his quarterstaff flying through the air like a spear, but Ashmedai leaps to the ground and the spear pierces the tree. Ashmedai slips something free of his pocket, and expecting a weapon, I throw a Saint Knife at him.

With a final grin, he disappears in a whirl of black smoke, my blade sinking uselessly into the earth.

I dismiss both knives and fight to catch my breath as Anna and Henry emerge, stepping gingerly over the ravaged ground. Salem hardly looks like he's broken a sweat as he dismisses his quarterstaff. The kind of power he just displayed, the strength—I want to be able to protect people like that. If it means leaving Ravenfall to do it, then maybe I have to.

"Yes," I tell him before I can second-guess my decision. "I want to be your apprentice."

A slow smile fills his face. "I'm very glad to hear that. We'll talk to your brother together when we get back."

Before I can reply, Anna grabs my arm, dragging me away a few paces so Henry and Salem can't hear. They're already discussing something, Henry gesturing angrily, while Salem clenches his jaw.

"What do you mean, apprentice?" Anna asks, pulling my attention back to her. "Liam's training you, with Aunt Elaine and Uncle Roy."

"Liam's always coming and going." I fold my arms. "So are your aunt and uncle. And unlike Liam, Salem actually *wants* to train me. I'm tired of feeling like a chore Liam has to scratch off his list. I want a real mentor."

"But . . ." She trails off. I can't think of the last time Anna

Ballinkay was at a loss for words, and it makes me falter. "I don't want you to go," she says at last.

"Salem said he'd stay at Ravenfall for a while," I tell her, starting to feel guilty. I hadn't really thought about what leaving would feel like. Turns out it feels a lot like betraying your best friend. But this is something that I have to do if I ever want to become a real Raven. "After that, once Salem teaches me how to be a Raven, I can come back. It won't be forever."

But she's already shaking her head. "Don't go with him, Colin. Something isn't right."

My growing guilt evaporates, replaced by annoyance. "What are you talking about?"

"Salem!" she hisses, glancing over at him as if he might hear, but he and Henry are absorbed in their own argument. "He's doing something to you."

My anger builds. "He's not—you don't know what you're talking about."

"Neither do you!"

"More than you do!"

A sharp thud cuts off my response. I look down to see a knife sticking out of the ground by my feet. A moment later, something shimmers into view. It's a thin, red snake, its scales glowing like fading embers.

Salem throws another knife into the ground and a second snake appears. "Fire serpents," he says. "Ashmedai left them when he fled, hoping to sow discord among us. They're known to stoke anger."

Sure enough, my bubbling annoyance cools with the snakes gone, but it doesn't go away completely. From the look on Anna's face, hers hasn't either, and Henry is rubbing the back of his neck with a bashful grimace.

"Come on," Salem says. "A walk will do us all some good."

That night, I toss and turn, dreaming of fiery serpents and worms that can destroy with a single look. I dream of my parents, too, the day I returned to our motel room to find Fin and his wraith standing over their bodies. How helpless I'd been, how powerless.

I wake biting back their names and roll over, wishing Max were there to comfort me. He still hasn't returned from his trip to visit the other Jabberwockies. I know he'll be able to find us when he wants; I just wish he was here now.

I blink, realizing the small shrub I've been staring at isn't a shrub after all. Rather, it's a small man, only a few inches high with pointed ears and a thick white beard, a drooping cap set atop his head. He holds a thimble-sized bowl of milk in his hands.

On instinct, I summon a Saint Knife, spinning up into a crouch. The creature yelps, nearly spilling his bowl of milk as he scurries back to the safety of the foliage.

"Please don't hurt me!" he calls in a thick Scottish accent from among the briar. "I only meant to make an offering, my lord."

"A . . . what?" I lower my blade, my mind catching up to my eyes. The man peers out from behind a tangle of leaves.

"You're a brownie," I realize aloud. A faerie of Scottish folk-lore known to complete household tasks for people in exchange for a bowl of milk. So then why is he bringing *me* one?

The brownie emerges fully from the bush and bows. "I am Balfour, my lord, and this clearing is my home."

I wince, glancing over my shoulder at the camp. The others are still asleep, but for how long? If Salem hears me chatting with a faerie, he's not going to like it. Especially not with a faerie who keeps calling me *my lord*.

"Stop saying that," I hiss. "My name is Colin."

Balfour bows again. "My Lord Colin."

I groan. "What do you want?" The quicker I can make him leave, the better.

Balfour holds up his bowl of milk. "As I said, my lord, to make an offering, and thank you for visiting my humble abode." He bows low, holding out the tiny bowl of milk to me. When I don't take it, he peers up at me, his brow furrowing. "Does it not please you, my lord? I beg your pardon. I wish only to be in your good graces when you ascend the throne."

"The *throne*?" I choke out. "I'm not ascending any throne. I'm not—" *Fin.*

The brownie begins to look uneasy. "Are you not the king, my lord? Descendant of the great Fin Varra? I heard tales you defeated the last king and took his power."

"That's not what happened." I glance back at the camp again. Salem doesn't know about my ancestry. What would he think of

150

me being descended from the King of the Dead? A *fae god,* not so different from Saoirse. There's no way he'll still want me as his apprentice.

I hold out my hand. "I'll accept your offering. But please, go."

Balfour bows again, placing the bowl in my hand. It's barely bigger than the tip of my finger. Then he backs away, keeping his head lowered, and flees into the underbrush.

I breathe a sigh of relief, sinking back into my sleeping bag and dismissing my knife. That was close.

"Colin?" Salem's voice snakes through the dark, and I nearly jump.

I peer over to find him standing at the edge of camp, fully dressed with his boots on. I look to his sleeping bag, which is lumped up as if someone still slept in it. He hadn't been there the whole time, which means—

"What is it?" I ask nervously, sure he's about to say he heard everything.

But he only jerks his head back the way he came. "I caught another creature trying to sneak into our camp."

My shoulders sink with relief, and I quickly pour out the thimble of milk where Salem can't see before hiding the cup in my sleeping bag. A couple minutes later, I'm dressed and following Salem into the woods, where a thick layer of snow has settled on the branches. Our wards kept our camp clear, but my boots now crunch with every step.

A soft orange glow bobs ahead of us. I expect to find another fire, only to see a large bird trussed up at the base of a tree. Its feathers are a muted red orange, like the tail end of a sunset, and it holds one of its wings limply and at an odd angle.

"Is that . . . a firebird?" I ask in awe.

"It is." Salem folds his arm, looking disappointed at my reaction. I quickly smother it. "I suspect it's another fiery servant of Ashmedai's."

I flinch, thinking of the snakes and how easily they stoked my anger. What havoc could a firebird wreak?

Salem summons a silver knife and offers it to me. "Lesson number one: never pass up an opportunity to stop a monster. A creature you leave undealt with today will only become a larger problem in the future, and you'll be responsible for whatever damage it does in the meantime."

I take the blade on reflex, the handle cool against my palm, and approach the firebird. It sits with its head hung low, its feathers pulsing with a dying light. The ropes binding it are silver too. The metal must be muting its magic, keeping it trapped.

The firebird looks up at me with pale gold eyes, and my already shaky determination falters. This isn't like Saoirse, who was threatening Anna's and Henry's lives. The firebird is defenseless and as far as I know, it hasn't done anything wrong. But that's exactly the kind of thinking that led to the púca getting away. For all I know, the púca led Ashmedai straight to us in the Crypt, and the firebird could do the same.

"Don't be fooled by its innocent look," Salem warns. "These creatures decimate homes and forests with their flames, and this one is likely an agent of Ashmedai. If given the chance, it will try to kill us."

My hand tightens on the blade. I know this is a test, that if I don't pass it, Salem might not want to train me anymore. He wants me to prove that I'm ready to be a real Raven, and this is what real Ravens do: hunt. But then why is my stomach squirming?

"Do what you're meant to, Colin," Salem says intently. "Show me why I should train you."

I lift the blade, and the firebird bows its head as if accepting its fate.

"Stop!" Anna's voice cuts through the night. She runs forward, placing herself between me and the firebird with her arms outstretched. "Colin, what are you doing? Firebirds aren't dangerous."

"Yes, they are!" Salem rounds on her. "I've seen what they can do firsthand. Watched their flames consume acres of land. How many have you met, Anna?"

Her expression falters. "None. But the stories—"

"Are just that," Salem says. At Anna's back, the firebird begins to struggle, likely sensing the possibility of freedom. "I'm trying to protect you. To protect everyone. Can't you see that?"

She hesitates, and I steel myself again. "Move out of the way, Anna. I have to do this."

"No, you don't." Her voice turns pleading. "Listen to me, Colin, this isn't you."

My jaw clenches. "I'm a Raven. This is exactly who I am."

She shakes her head, and the firebird struggles more fiercely. "Ravens protect life. They don't take it."

My frustration hits a boiling point and I shout, "Stop acting like you know what's best for me! You're just as bad as Liam, trying to tell me what to do all the time. It's my life, Anna. My choices."

My boot comes down on a stray crimson feather, and the magic that's been sleeping inside me whirls to life. It feels exactly the same as the day I used it to bring Max back from the brink of death, moments after Fin revealed that I'd inherited a sliver of his power.

The magic latches on to the life left in the firebird's feather, and my vision shifts. One moment I'm looking at the bound creature, the next I see it soaring through violet skies, embers of light trailing in its wake. The vision changes, showing me another sky and a landscape of snow-capped peaks. Then a winding forest river with a sky of stars.

A hundred skies, a hundred lifetimes, the firebird burning up to cinders after each one and rising again from the ashes. It lives peacefully in solitude, until humans begin to encroach on its land, taking forests and polluting streams. It's chased from home to home, forced to defend itself with flame, until finally the human world grew too small, and it came here hoping for safety and quiet.

Distantly, I know this isn't normal, that a Raven shouldn't be able to do this. This is Fin's power, a new aspect I've never experienced before.

Soon you won't be able to touch someone without their life magic invading you. Saoirse's words come flying back to me, and I pull free of the vision with a sudden gasp. My head jerks toward Salem—how long was I gone? Does he suspect anything? But Salem's eyes are on the firebird, a warning rising to his lips. Too late, I turn as the silver ropes tear apart and the firebird thrusts out its wings, taking to the sky.

I throw my knife after it on reflex, but it goes wide, and the creature vanishes into the night.

Salem gives me a disappointed look. "You said you wanted to be my apprentice, Colin."

"I do—"

"Then stop hesitating." His narrowed gaze shifts briefly to Anna before he strikes out back for camp. "Figure out what you want."

With the firebird gone, I can barely see Anna in the moonlight, but there's enough for me to make out her gutted expression. I refuse to look sorry, even if part of me wilts with relief. The firebird had just been looking for a home, a feeling I know well, but surely that vision hadn't been its whole story? Salem wouldn't have captured it if it was.

"What is wrong with you?" Anna demands. "That firebird did nothing to us!"

I summon back my Saint Knife and dismiss it. "It's a dangerous magical creature, Anna. It had to be stopped." Despite my confidence, the words feel wrong. But I'm sure that it's what Salem would say.

She throws up her hands. "Stopped from what? Being a giant floating lantern? Because that's all it was doing!"

"For now," I hiss back. "Salem said it tried to get into our camp. For all we know it's working for Ashmedai and it's off to tell him our location right now."

She shakes her head in disbelief. "Why won't you listen to me? I'm just worried about you."

"No, you're getting in the way," I say through gritted teeth. "Salem's just trying to prepare me to be a Raven, and you keep ruining it."

"He's wrong about the firebird—"

"Salem is an adult! A Raven!" I throw up my hands. "He knows more than you about this. You're just jealous again."

Hurt flashes across her face, and I wince, at once wanting to take it back and not. Then her expression hardens. "No, I'm not," she says determinedly. "Salem's messing with your head. He's not good for you, but you take everything he says as law. Kill this, Colin, kill that. Be a jerk to your best friend because that's what heroes do. Well, guess what? It's not!"

"You wouldn't know! He's making me strong, Anna. He's—" I cut off, swallowing back a sudden flood of emotion. "He's like what I imagine my dad would have been like, if he were here to train me."

I don't realize how much I mean that until I say it. Salem has so many qualities I loved about my dad—intelligence, capability, leadership. He's not as funny, or as soft, and I can't imagine him in the kitchen cooking all afternoon, but he's *here* and that's more than I can say for my father.

My father, who lied to me and kept me in the dark, just like my mom. Just like Liam. They didn't trust me to be able to handle the truth, and it got them killed, and nearly me along with them.

If they'd let me make my own decision, if they'd taught me to use my powers, everything could have been different.

I won't make their same mistake. Things *will* be different.

"He's not your dad, Colin," Anna says gently. "You don't even know him that well."

I sneer, a retort rising to my lips before I can think. "Who are you to talk about knowing people? You think you and your dad are best friends, but he barely notices you!"

Anna recoils, a look on her face that makes me want to take every word back, to throw a knife into the ground and expose the fiery serpent that made me say them—but the only snake here is me.

Tears break from Anna's eyes, and she turns, fleeing back to camp.

Ravenfall

"Okay," Roy says, staring out the kitchen window at the snowy Hollowthorn Woods. "They definitely moved."

Elaine rolls her eyes, hands clasped around an eggnog latte. "Thank you for your astute observation."

The trees have covered nearly half the frosted lawn, leaving trails of flattened grass in their wake. The house can feel them reaching, coming closer, trying to draw it in. They aren't hostile, but they feel desperate, and the house doesn't understand what's happening. It doesn't know how to help.

A scream sounds from the foyer, and Roy and Elaine burst out of the kitchen to find a woman swatting wildly at her hair. A green forest pixie clings to one curl, likely intending to use her hair as its new nest—except forest pixies never come inside.

The house never *lets* them inside.

It reaches for its wards while Roy and Elaine help free the

woman from the pixie. They're there, but faint. Weak enough that anything could enter if it wanted to. How dare that pixie take advantage of its weakened state! Wards or not, it should know better. The house has stood for hundreds of years, and it will stand hundreds more before it lets a pixie boss it around.

But as the house reaches deeper into its magic, intending to send the pixie on its way, it senses something else. A gnawing, frantic presence pressing, pressing, pressing. It realizes then that the woods are much closer than it thought. It feels a root prying at the outside staircase, feels it drawing from the magic there.

"That's it!" yells the woman as Roy frees the pixie and shoos it out a nearby window. "First the water that smelled like pine trees, then that terrible groaning in the attic, now this? This place is falling apart. I'm leaving!"

"Ma'am, if you would just—" Elaine cuts off as the woman bolts back up the stairs to pack.

Roy runs a frustrated hand through his hair. "*Now* do we call Nora?"

"If we bring her back now, she'll never leave the inn again," Elaine fires back.

The woman isn't the last to go. Over the course of the afternoon, every last guest at Ravenfall checks out, citing doorways that open into forests and windows that look out on impossibly blue rivers singing lilting songs. There are gnomes in another's dresser and a púca sleeping on a man's pillow, leaves coming out of the faucets and snow falling from the ceiling.

When the last of the guests have gone and it is only Roy and

Elaine and the house, it makes a last effort to warn them, to tell them that the wood is coming for them all, desperate for their aid. It needs them for something. Needs them to fix something, to stop something—the house can't tell which it is.

But it needs their help, and it will do whatever it takes to get it.

CHAPTER 16

Anna

I fall asleep crying and wake up feeling numb.

Colin's never said anything like that to me. We've argued before, but never fought, not like that. I wish I never said anything. Maybe then everything would be okay, and I wouldn't feel like my stomach is clenched in a fist. Even Kara's never made me feel this bad.

When I clamber out of my sleeping bag, camp is already packed up, the remains of a fire smoldering. Henry and Salem are talking quietly to each other, with Colin nowhere to be seen. I hate how relieved I am at that. I don't want to face him.

"Anna." Henry calls me over, and I join them, realizing Salem is holding the Myrtle Staff. My instinct is to grab it back from him, but he hands it to me as I join them. The look on his face tells me he's still upset with me for last night too.

"Can you tell how close we are?" he asks.

I take the staff, diving into the magic. The tree's presence is nearly overwhelming now, and I quickly retreat and say, "Really close. Just over that way," and point.

"Good." Salem takes the staff back from me, though I'm reluctant to let him. "Henry and I have been talking, and we've decided it's best that you and he don't travel any farther with us."

I start. "What?"

"Ashmedai is probably going to attack again," Henry says more gently. "It's his last chance to take the staff before we return it to the tree. If Colin and Salem have to worry about protecting us and defending the staff, they're only going to get hurt. Besides, we've done our part: we got them here with the staff."

"But—" I stop, not knowing what to say. *But I think Salem's messing with Colin's head and making him do things?*

I already tried talking to Henry about this once and he didn't listen. No one is listening, and I don't know what to do about it. What if I'm wrong about all of this, and *I'm* the problem? I might not agree with some of Colin's decisions, but what has Salem really done except keep us safe and risk his life to protect the tree from Ashmedai? He's been my dad's friend for years. How would I feel if someone suddenly said Colin was dangerous?

Guilt prickles my insides, and I toe a nearby rock with my shoe. I probably owe Colin an apology, but I don't really feel sorry. Because deep down, I know I'm right. Something is off about Salem. I don't trust him, and I'm worried about Colin. Now Salem wants us to stay behind while he and Colin go ahead?

"I've set up the ward perimeter." Salem waves to the four lantern-like objects surrounding the camp, his silver ring glinting in the filtered sunlight. "Also, I can sense Max is nearby. Wait here where you're safe until he either arrives to escort you home, or we come back from returning the staff to the tree. If you go, just leave our packs here. They'll be safe inside the wards."

Relief shoots through me at hearing Max is close. At least he'll be on my side.

"Where's Colin?" I ask, thinking he'll agree that we shouldn't be left behind, even after our argument last night. We always do things like this together.

"Patrolling," Salem replies with a look that tells me he knows exactly what I'm thinking. Did he plan this so Colin wouldn't be here to argue too? "I'll meet up with him and we'll head for the tree. Stay inside the wards."

"Good luck," Henry says, and Salem nods before starting for the woods, pausing only briefly to activate the wards.

It's only once the trees swallow him up that my despair hits me full force. My hands clench into fists, trembling. We were supposed to do this together. Does Colin know what Salem's doing? Does he care, or does he agree with Salem that we're just a distraction?

"Well, I call that a successful expedition," Henry says, pulling his logbook out of his pocket to make a notation.

"Is that all you care about?" My voice breaks. Henry blinks at me in surprise, and I say, "All you ever talk about is magical objects. You're never home and you never pay attention to me. I don't even know who you are!"

"Anna—"

But I don't listen, running as far as I can to the other side of the camp. Everything Colin said last night is true. My dad and I aren't close, we never have been, and there's a part of me that is a little jealous of Colin and Salem. Salem might be intense, but he cares about Colin and spends time with him.

All Henry cares about is magical objects.

The bushes beyond the ward rattle, and I jerk out of my thoughts. Sticks snap, leaves shuddering, as something runs straight toward our camp.

I back away, looking for a weapon. What if Ashmedai has been waiting for Colin and Salem to leave so he can capture us and use us against them?

A shape barrels out of the nearest bush and into the clearing—small, black, and leaking silver blood.

"Max!" I drop to my knees beside him. There are burns around his ankles and muzzle, and several scratches that have stopped bleeding. "What happened to you?"

He looks around me, searching for something, and when he doesn't find it, the panic in his bright green eyes doubles.

"Are you looking for Colin and Salem?" I ask. "They went ahead to the tree."

Max lets out a low, keening sound, more Jabberwocky than cat. He paces before me, jittery and on edge in a way I've never seen him. Jabberwockies and Ravens have a unique connection, which is why I believed Salem when he said Max was on his way back. But if Salem really sensed him, he would have known Max was injured. Did he know and not say anything, or had he not really checked for Max at all?

"Anna!" Henry sprints over to us with a look of alarm and crouches by my side, his logbook abandoned by his pack. "What happened?"

"I don't know." Not for the first time, I wish Max could actually speak.

Except I know the next best thing.

"Max," I say. "Can I read you?"

If he lets me use my psychometry on him, I can see what happened to him, and maybe then I'll understand.

Max goes still, a look in his eye that it takes me a moment to recognize: fear.

I've never seen Max afraid of anything.

For a moment, I actually think he's going to bolt, but then the tension washes out of him, and he comes to sit before me, head bowed.

I hesitate, not sure I want to see what could make Max so terrified, but I can't ignore this either. Henry gives me a reassuring nod, and I steel myself. Placing my hand atop Max's head, I begin building a bridge.

It's so easy I barely have to try. I know Max almost as well as I know myself. Or so I thought—because I'm not ready for the flood of unfamiliar memories that comes rushing in.

I see Salem through Max's eyes, but he's young, maybe Liam's age. They're on a hunt together, working alongside each other like Ravens and Jabberwockies often do.

Together they take down a vampire that's been terrorizing Salem's hometown. Except when they emerge from the woods and back into town, it looks like nowhere I've ever seen before.

The buildings are made of stone and closely packed together, the streets cobblestone. It looks like Ireland or England—except instead of cars, there are horse-drawn carriages, and women in big, pleated dresses like ballgowns. It's a picture out of my history textbooks come to life.

The memory shifts to Salem standing before two graves. Max is on his shoulder, and I can feel his pain, how much he cares about Salem and wants him to be happy.

Another shift, and they're hunting again. Salem is exhausted but he won't stop, demanding to go on hunt after hunt.

Shift, and I see Max coming upon Salem as he kills a sleeping púca. Again and again, he hunts down defenseless creatures that haven't hurt anyone.

Max is worried. He tries to make Salem stop but Salem won't listen.

Another shift, and Salem's older. He looks more like how I know him. He's on an expedition with some others, keeping them safe. They find what they're after—a vial of ambrosia, the nectar of the gods. The people of the expedition fight over it, each wanting the nectar's power, which promises a longer life.

But Salem is stronger than them, and he doesn't hesitate to hurt them and take the vial.

It's not the last time. Several more memories flash through, showing other times Salem went searching for ways to live longer. He travels the world, seeking out experts to help him locate powerful objects and rare magic, and everywhere he goes, people and creatures get hurt. Max tries to stop him, to bring him back to himself, but it's no use.

The setting changes, and I recognize Wick. It looks a little different, some of the buildings missing or different colors, and I wonder how far in the past this is.

Salem hunts down a local witch for a poultice said to extend life. Max tries to stop him, but Salem kills her and steals the poultice before Max can intervene. Horrified, Max refuses to help him anymore.

Salem severs their bond, leaving Max stranded without a connection to magic.

He's dying when the witch's sister finds him and takes him to Ravenfall. I recognize her olive skin and long coils of dark hair—my Bubbe, Henry's mother. She gives Max to a young-faced Gran, and he bonds with the house's magic. In return, he changes the house's hats each morning and keeps its people safe.

Everything turns, and then Salem is walking through the door at Ravenfall, except I see myself standing by the stairs, years younger than I am now. I feel Max's surprise, his pain—his hope. Salem's here to help Henry on an expedition. He pulls Max aside and tells him, "I'm not who I was. I've changed. Made amends."

Max wants to believe him. He wants his old friend to be better, to be the boy he once knew.

The expedition goes fine. Max hears nothing of Salem's anger, his violence. He starts to believe he's changed, holds on to that hope when Salem returns to Ravenfall again seeking their help with Ashmedai. But then Salem starts sneaking out of camp only days into their journey. He starts stoking Colin's anger and manipulating him.

Max confronts him, and Salem warns, "If you say anything, I'll tell them what you did. Everything you did by my side. They'll hate you. They'll reject you."

I feel Max's shame when he stays quiet.

Then Max follows Salem one night into the woods. He comes upon him talking to someone, planning—

I nearly jerk out of the vision with surprise.

It's Ashmedai.

Salem catches Max watching. He wounds him and binds him with silver cord, leaving him trussed to a tree. Something must remain between them, as he leaves Max alive.

"You never did understand, old friend," Salem says. "I have a duty to protect, and I will do what I must to see it through."

I come up from the vision gasping for air. Henry is by my side, asking if I'm okay, but I can't find the words. Max is quivering. I can still feel his fear, his pain, his shame, but also his resolve to tell the truth. To be responsible for what he did and stop it from happening again.

Silently, I gather him into my arms, holding him close until he stills. He never told us any of this. All the times I touched him before I learned to control my powers, he hid his memories of death from me, ashamed of what he'd done and worried that we'd reject him if we found out.

"You're my family, Max," I tell him, holding tight. "I'd never give up on you."

Just like I can't give up on Colin.

Max bops his head against mine and I squeeze him one last time before letting go. He wobbles a little, but when I give him a concerned look, he only lifts his head, ready to move.

I nod to him and stand, facing Henry. "Salem has been hunting down sources of immortality for hundreds of years," I say, and explain everything I saw in my vision. I feel sick with every word I speak. "He's controlling Ashmedai. He used us to get the Myrtle Staff and find the Tree of Life so that he can become immortal."

"My aunt . . ." Henry trails off, thoughts of the witch Salem killed clouding his face. "My mother never told us what happened to her."

I squeeze his hand, and his fingers curl around mine. He takes a deep breath. "If you're right, then the Seal of Solomon . . ." He pulls the fake ring out of his pocket. "Salem must have the real one. It's the only way he'd be able to command Ashmedai. He must have found it before I did and replaced the original with a replica."

My heart drops to my stomach as everything we've learned really settles. I was right.

Colin's in danger.

CHAPTER 17

Colin

"Where are the others?" I ask when Salem joins me in the woods. I've been thinking over how I'm going to apologize to Anna all morning. I'm still kind of upset with her, but what I said was really mean and she didn't deserve it. She was only looking out for me, like we always do for each other, and instead of talking to her about it, I blew up.

It's not even her fault. I'm just angry all the time, and I don't know how to make it stop. It feels like it's burning me up from the inside out, and now it's scorching everyone around me too. When this is over, I'll apologize to her for real.

"They decided to stay behind," Salem replies. "We agreed they might get in the way if they came."

I glance back toward camp. "But will they be safe there? Without Max—"

"They'll be fine. Do you really think I'd leave them there if I thought they were in danger?"

I wither beneath Salem's sharp gaze. "No, sorry."

Salem holds up the Myrtle Staff. "We're close enough now that I can feel the tree's magic through the staff. I should be able to guide us the rest of the way."

I fall in step alongside him, anticipation building in my stomach. This time, I'll finally be able to show Salem what I'm capable of.

"What's our plan once we reach the tree?" I ask, stepping over a fallen log.

"We return the staff to the tree before Ashmedai arrives," Salem replies with an edge of annoyance.

"What if he finds us and tries to stop us?"

"Then we defeat him."

"How—"

Salem's frown cuts me off. "If you don't know how to kill a demon, then maybe you aren't worthy of being my apprentice after all."

"Silver," I mutter, irked, but if Salem hears me, he doesn't acknowledge it. I try not to let his terseness get to me. He's probably just on edge and trying to prepare for the coming battle, the same thing I should be doing instead of asking questions.

As we walk, the air begins to change. The magic grows thicker, taking on an almost honey-sweet scent. The trees become denser, the ground covered in a thick layer of leaves, until we reach a line of willows with long feathery branches that block what lies beyond.

"We're here." Salem's knuckles are nearly white where he grasps the staff. I look up, expecting to be able to see the tree through the tight canopy above, but there's only pieces of sky. Elaine said the tree has a natural glamour that prevents people from seeing it until they've reached it, but what defines *reached*?

Salem parts the willow branches with the staff, dissolving the glamour. "The Tree of Life."

A wide glade spreads out before us, waves of verdant grass rolling up to the roots of an impossible tree. It's unlike anything I've ever seen before. The trunk is so wide I can't see end to end, the bark a rich walnut color at first glance. But when I look closer, I realize there's actually bark of every kind, from gray oak to pale birch to the same myrtle of the staff. I recognize them easily after so much time around Rose.

Above, the canopy stretches for what feels like forever, encompassing the whole of the realm. It's so high it looks like the sky, and parts of it are blanketed with stars and small suns, and I wonder if we ever really saw the sky here, or if we've only ever been staring up at this tree.

Birds flit in and out of branches heavy with fruit of every kind, and I hear the distant rush of several rivers trailing away from its roots. The grassland forms a perfect circle around the trunk, each blade of grass an impossibly full green before it meets the forest again on every side.

I take a step back, glancing up through the canopy again, but there's only sky, no sign of the tree. But when I move forward back to the edge of the willow, the tree stretches above me in all its glory.

"It's incredible," I breathe as we enter the massive glade.

I look to Salem, a grin breaking across my face, only to find him staring at the tree with an intense look of hunger. It's out of place on his normally cool features, and I have the sudden urge to step away from him.

"Salem?" I ask uncertainly.

He blinks, coming back to himself. "Yes, it is. Come on, let's get closer."

With every step we take toward the tree, a feeling in my chest grows stronger. It reminds me of when I first got my Raven powers, when the magic flowed through me, and I know that it's the sliver of Fin's power calling for my attention, the same way it overcame me with the firebird.

Fin was the King of the Dead—and before us is the Tree of Life. It makes sense that his magic would be stronger here. Strong enough that I struggle to keep it in check, to force it down where it can't be a part of me.

I'm so close to proving myself to Salem—I won't let Fin take that from me too.

"This tree is the source of so much power," Salem says as we near the roots. "With its strength, we could eradicate every last supernatural creature in existence."

"All of them?" I ask, thinking about Max, and Elra, the little pocket dragon that helps mind the Andrade Animal Shelter in downtown Wick. I think of Mrs. Andrade herself, who is a kelpie, and Balfour, the brownie who brought me the thimble of milk that I tossed away so carelessly.

"All of them," Salem says with a sudden fervor. "Think about it, Colin. There'd be no more death, no more destruction. No one else will have to grow up like you and I did, wishing they could have done more."

An uneasy feeling begins to gather in my stomach. "But what about the ones that aren't evil?"

"They're all evil." Salem's voice goes cold. "Every single one of them. They're all monsters."

I slow to a stop, and Salem looks back at me with a frown. A question I can't ignore presses warningly at the back of my mind, and I ask hesitantly, "Salem . . . where's Max?"

"With the other Jabberwockies, as I said," he replies, but it comes out stiff.

"Then why isn't he back yet?" I press. "He wouldn't have left us on our own for so long."

Salem starts to respond, then pauses, releasing a heavy sigh as though he'd hoped to spare me knowing this. "The truth is, Max stuck his nose where it didn't belong."

My stomach swoops, and I take a step back. Salem gives me a sympathetic look. "These are the hard choices we have to make as Ravens. Sometimes that means doing difficult things in order to do the right thing."

"But Max . . ." I can't find the words. Would Salem really have done something terrible to him? Ravens and Jabberwockies are on the same side. We have been for centuries.

The magic in my gut begins to stir, responding to the flurry of confusion and concern building inside me. Something cracks, and I reach into my pocket to find the amethyst leaf I took from the Gemstone Forest in pieces. Like a vacuum unsealing, I suddenly hear the ghostly whisper of voices, feel the press of spirits nearby, and see the near-solid figure of the grinning redcap. But the strongest feeling—it's coming from Salem.

He closes the distance between us. "Listen to me, Colin. I want to share my power with you, to teach you everything that I know and make you the Raven you want to be. But it won't be easy. I need you to trust me. Can you do that?"

He holds his hand out to me, an offering.

I take it, his ring pressing into my fingers—and finally open myself to Fin's power, reaching deep into the well of magic that's been waiting inside me.

It courses through me like a cool wave of mist. Between one blink and another, everything changes, like sliding on a pair of colored glasses. The world takes on a bluish tint, and I see the spirits around us, the souls too weak to make themselves visible and the bright flare of the redcap. I hear their voices, but I push them away and look to Salem.

A bright silver light outlines him, and in the center of his chest is a dark, roiling mass. It crackles with red energy that feels as if it's decaying, and I realize with a sickening feeling that it's his soul.

It's existed far longer than it should, now corrupt with external magic, dark magic, that's kept him alive for centuries.

Then I understand.

When I release his hand, I take his silver ring with me. He shouts, but I leap back, putting space between us. The glamour on the ring falls away, the silver turning to brass. A pentagram appears on the face of it.

The Seal of Solomon.

"You lied," I croak. "Ashmedai was never after the tree. You've been controlling him. It's been you this entire time!"

Anger floods Salem's face with color. "I do what I must to protect people!"

I shake my head, closing my hand around the ring. How could I have missed this? I'm supposed to keep people safe, to defend against danger, but the danger's been right beside me this entire time.

"You're not protecting anyone," I say. "You just want the tree's power for yourself so you can live forever."

"So I can *hunt* forever," Salem corrects. "Don't you understand, Colin? If I take the tree's magic, the Otherworld will die. All these creatures will be gone, and all that will be left are the ones already in the human world. We can hunt them down one by one until there's nothing left to threaten us."

"Magic will die too," I say. "Innocent creatures and people whose livelihoods depend on it."

Ravenfall would cease to exist, its magic drained from it.

Would Anna and her family keep their powers? Did *they* fall into Salem's category of those who had to be removed?

"Anna was right," I say, hating myself for not listening to her. I've been so caught up in earning Salem's approval that I didn't see what was right in front of me. "You were just using me."

"I will not be judged by the likes of you, son of Fin," he snaps.

I recoil, and Salem's snarl turns into a sneer. "Oh yes, I know what you are. I thought I could mold you in spite of your heritage, make you something better than the half-baked offspring of a forgotten god. But you're just like him, aren't you? A monster."

"I'm not!" I say, desperate for it to be true. But look how easily I gave in to my anger, to Fin's power. I let them both control me. What if he's right? What if there's more of Fin in me than I want to admit?

"I offered to share my power with you," Salem says grimly. "Remember that."

Then he slams the Myrtle Staff into the nearest tree root. It comes alight with magic, funneling out of the tree and along the staff into Salem as he absorbs the tree's magic. It wafts off him in a silver mist, his skin encased in a layer of light as some of the vibrance of the tree begins to fade.

I do the first thing I can think of and summon the staff back to my journal. It vanishes from his hand, and he rounds on me with a roar of anger and surprise, summoning a set of silver knives. "You linked it?"

"Anna never trusted you, and she was right," I say as I slip the

Seal of Solomon onto my finger. Its power zips through me, and I yell, "Ashmedai!"

A swirl of black smoke erupts at my side, dispersing to reveal the grinning demon. He performs a mock clap. "Bravo, little Raven." His gaze slants to Salem. "I did warn you not to play with your food. But alas, no one ever listens to my advice."

"Be silent, demon," Salem snaps.

But Ashmedai only laughs. "You hold the ring no longer."

"I do." I straighten, then command, "Hold him off."

Ashmedai tilts his head, his body straining for a brief moment, before a mocking smile curls his lips. "Oh, you'll have to try harder than that, fledgling. This is powerful magic, and I don't think you're strong enough to use it."

"You're playing with forces you don't understand," Salem warns, holding out a hand. "Give that back before you get hurt."

"I could say the same of you," I hiss, backing toward the tree. If I can just return the staff to the tree, this will all be over.

Salem's snarl curves into an understanding smile. "Foolish boy. The staff cannot be returned to the tree. I only told you that so Anna would help me bring it here."

I flinch—another lie. We could have taken the staff back with us to Ravenfall this entire time or given it to a whole host of Ravens to guard while we tracked down Ashmedai—except the demon was never our opponent.

"Now give me the staff!" Salem shouts, and shoots toward me.

I try to dismiss Ashmedai—except nothing happens. He waves at me with a grin and vanishes into smoke. Then Salem is there. I only just summon my Saint Knives in time to block his attack. His strength is nearly overpowering, shoving me back, and I barely manage to dodge his next swing.

Smoke erupts in my face, and Ashmedai seizes my wrist, his claws digging into my skin. "My ring, if you please."

I squeeze my hand into a fist so he can't remove the ring and swing at him with my other blade. He vanishes again, and Salem barrels through the smoke, slashing a shallow line along my arm. I counter, but he leaps back. He barely lands before he's on me again, Ashmedai harrying me from the other side to get the ring, and I know in that moment: I can't win this fight.

Not alone.

Ravenfall

Something is very, very wrong.

There are roots moving beneath the house's foundation. Roots crawling in its walls and threatening to explode into rooms. Roots climbing over its many faces, leaving trails of sticky sap and gouging the stone.

The house shudders violently, waking Roy and Elaine in their rooms. When Roy rolls over to go back to sleep, it tilts his bed, throwing him out.

It's the last bit of magic the house can bear to do.

A tree rips through the floorboards and skewers Roy's now empty bed. He yelps, scrambling to his feet and going for the ax in his weapons cupboard. The house can't open it for him, so it watches him scramble for the right combination and rip the ax free. He holds it up in one hand, a flame coming alight in the other, but the tree doesn't attack.

"Roy!" Elaine throws open his door, a cut on her cheek the house didn't see happen. It checks her room and finds it crawling with roots and vines that must have nearly swallowed her. The house couldn't protect her.

It can't protect anyone now.

"What in all the worlds is happening?" Roy demands, clutching his ax.

"Hollowthorn Woods is swallowing the house," Elaine replies as if she can't quite believe her own words. "I barely sensed it in time to escape. And the house—it isn't fighting back."

The house *can't* fight back.

It wants to tell them that it is trying. Wants to tell them that the wood is only asking for help, that something is happening in the Otherworld that it desperately wants to stop. That the house and the trees have been one for so long, even after they were separated, that it was the only place the wood could think to come for help.

But the wood has taken back the magic that it once gave to the house, taken it and left it powerless.

So when the roots rip through Roy's room, wrapping around him and Elaine like snakes, the house can't do anything but watch.

CHAPTER 18

Anna

"Hurry!" I take off in the direction Salem went, but when I reach the edge of the ward, my body goes still on its own. I try to fight my way forward, but I can't take a step over the line.

Henry pulls me back, looking between the two nearest lanterns. "These aren't keeping things out," he says. "They're keeping us *in.*"

"What do we do?" I ask as Max sniffs the nearest one and lets out a hiss.

Henry kneels next to the lantern. It's about a foot high, with a black metal frame and glass sides. There's something bright red at the lantern's center. Henry pulls out his logbook, flipping back through several pages until he finds the one he's looking for.

"I thought so," he says. "These are the same wards Salem used on our last expedition together years ago. I asked him about them then, and he said they were powered by gemstones gifted to him by a Jewish witch. By inscribing the stones with numerals representing words, she gave them power."

"Like the gate in the Crypt." I crouch down beside him. "So, what, we just remove the stone?"

"That should do it. Salem likely didn't account for us figuring out the truth, so I don't anticipate that he would have modified them to prevent tampering." Henry holds out an arm, pushing me back. "Give me space. I don't want you near here if it goes wrong."

I retreat reluctantly, but Max stays with Henry, his body already translucent in preparation to absorb any magic that gets released.

Henry pulls a small pickax-shaped tool out of his bag and hits the pointed end against the glass, shattering it. He reaches inside and pulls the gemstone free. Then, cautiously, he reaches across the ward line—and his hand passes through.

"You did it!" I say as Henry turns the crystal over in his hand.

"He reversed the spell," he says, showing me where the last inscription had been crossed out and a new one carved in. "From to keep out, to keep in."

I grab his hand, pulling him to his feet. "We can look at it later. Let's go!"

We take off into the woods, Max leading the way, likely following the feel of Colin's and Salem's magic. Henry huffs along beside me, and as a stitch locks into place in my side, I wish I'd spent more time running drills with Colin instead of drawing by the fire, but we keep running. Around us, the trees begin to groan, sounding almost pained. Their branches sway and rattle, shaking loose leaves and flutters of snow as if urging us onward.

Max jerks to a sudden stop, and I jump over him to keep from stepping on him.

"What is it?" I ask as he sniffs the air frantically one direction and then the next.

"It's probably the tree's glamour," Henry says in between pants. "Without the staff, we won't be able to see it until we're upon it. It must be impacting Max's ability to track Colin now that we're so close."

Max's frustrated snarl reverberates with the power of a Jabberwocky, and his body flickers in and out of sight. In a blink, he transforms and lifts his boxy head to the sky, sniffing again. Then he cocks his head. At first, I think he's caught the trail, but then he makes a high keening noise that sounds like the note of a song.

An answering call echoes from far off, and Max lets out another howl. As more voices join the chorus, I recognize the melancholy melody—he's talking to the other Jabberwockies!

The ground shudders, and I hear twigs snapping. Henry moves in front of me, but I peer around him, my heart jangling in my chest.

The tree branches above us rustle, and then a massive creature emerges from the brush. Easily twice the size of Max, the Jabberwocky's coat is a rich, full black, its tail studded with foot-long spikes. Dark, leathery wings shroud its back, and it stretches them high above its head.

Max returns the greeting, beating his wings once, then lowering his head. The other Jabberwocky sniffs him, and Henry and I both hold our breath. We might not speak Giant Magical Creature, but we both know Max is being measured right now.

At last, the other Jabberwocky gives a long cry, and Max lowers his wings. He makes a questioning noise, and the other Jabberwocky approaches us. It dips its head to our level, its long neck curving around us, and meets my gaze.

"Um, hi?" I offer. The Jabberwocky gives one slow blink that I hope doesn't mean *You're dinner.*

"Anna," Henry whispers. "I think it wants you to read it."

"Are you sure?" I eye the Jabberwocky's mouthful of fangs. "Because if you're wrong, you'll owe me a new hand."

Max keens encouragingly, and I peel myself free of Henry to face the other Jabberwocky. If this is the only way we can get to Colin in time, I don't have a choice.

"Here goes everything," I mutter, and set my hand on the Jabberwocky's head.

I don't have to build a bridge. The vision of the path to the tree erupts inside my head with utter clarity and ease, gifted by the Jabberwocky. In a blink, it's over, and the Jabberwocky pulls free. It gives Max one last chirrup, then transforms into a large raven and flaps away into the trees.

"I am never doing that again," I exhale, then point between two trees. "It's straight that way."

We take off along the path the Jabberwocky gave me. The vision is practically seared into my memory, and I remember every thick-trunked tree and sprawling bush we pass. A fallen log should be right . . . there! We leap over it, and just like in the vision, the trees grow denser and the ground turns to a carpet of leaves, until we reach the line of willows guarding the tree beyond. We break through their branches to enter an enormous glade.

The Tree of Life rises before us, stopping Henry in his tracks, but I only have eyes for the battle happening at its roots.

Salem drives an elbow into Colin's sternum, knocking the air out of his lungs. Colin wheezes and drops to his knees. In a flash of black smoke, Ashmedai appears, reaching for Colin's hand. The Seal of Solomon glints on his finger, but before Ashmedai can seize it, Salem strikes at the demon, forcing him to vanish again.

Somehow, Colin must have gotten the ring. But then why can't he control Ashmedai?

Salem slams a boot into Colin's chest, sending him sprawling onto his back. He reaches for the ring.

I don't hesitate—I launch myself straight at Salem, knocking into him. He flies back into the nearest root, his head hitting the wood.

"Anna!" Colin cries out in surprise. "How—"

I open my fist, showing him the jade leaves I took from the Gemstone Forest that grant strength. Or rather, what remains of them. I accidentally crushed them in my attack, and I let the pieces flutter to the ground.

"Come on." I grab his wrist. "We have to get out of here."

"But how?" He looks over to where Salem is already stirring. "We can't outrun him."

"We don't have to." We both turn as Henry arrives, pointing at another root. Max stands on it in full Jabberwocky form, twice as big as he normally is and fueled by the Otherworld's magic. His whole body shimmers with silver light, and I realize what Henry means.

Jabberwockies are creatures of the Shield. They help maintain the balance between life and death by assisting spirits crossing from the human world to the Otherworld, their bodies acting like portals when they turn incorporeal. But now we're in the Otherworld, and the balance is reversed: he can help humans cross back to the human world.

"Not with my ring, you don't," hisses a saccharine voice. Then Ashmedai is there again, a bright flame gathered in his palm.

Colin steps between us and brings his knives together in a powerful clang. The pure note rings through the glade, and Ashmedai cringes. He does it again, and the flame winks out as the demon presses a hand to his head.

"What is that infernal noise?" he demands.

Colin hits the knives a third time, and then lifts the hand with the ring. "Leave!" he commands.

Ashmedai snarls, lurching toward us—then vanishes in a puff of black smoke.

Colin's shoulders slump with exhaustion, and I take his hand as Salem clambers unsteadily to his feet. We make a run for Max, but when I glance over my shoulder, Henry isn't behind us. He's still next to Salem, scraping something into the stone he took from the lantern.

"The next time you come near my family, you don't get a warning," he says, and then thrusts the stone into Salem's chest.

Salem's eyes go wide, and then he crumples to the ground.

Henry sprints toward us. "Go!"

We don't need telling twice. Colin dismisses his Saint Knives, instead summoning his journal from his pack back in camp, and we run straight into Max, whose power pulls us through in a cold wave. Henry leaps through after us, and we all tumble to the forest floor in the Hollowthorn Woods, a canopy of real stars above us.

Then Max appears, still in his Jabberwocky form but solid once more. He sways, shrinking back to cat form, and then collapses in a heap.

CHAPTER 19

Colin

"Max!" I fall to my knees beside him, gathering him into my arms. Even transforming far away from the house can be too much for him. Doing what he just did—it's a miracle he's even still alive, especially with his body still healing from whatever Salem did to him. Though from his shallow, wheezing breath I don't think that he has long.

Anna hovers anxiously beside us. "You have to bond with him, Colin. Without a link to a Raven, he's not strong enough to survive."

Max cracks open one eye and tries to move, like he's attempting to slide free, but his energy runs out and he goes limp in my grasp.

"It's okay, Max," Anna says gently. "Colin will understand."

"Understand what?" I ask, and she bites her lip, looking to

Max. There's something I'm missing, but I don't have time to figure it out. Even so, I won't do this without Max's permission.

"Are you okay with this, Max?" I ask. "Bonding?"

He peers at me with one bright green eye, as if looking for something I can't see. Then he nods.

I dive into my magic, the same as I do when I'm linking an object to my journal. When I connect it to Max's, the two magics snap together, becoming one. We both start to glow with silver light, and with it comes a flood of thoughts and emotions, and a series of memories I can hardly keep up with.

Salem and Max hunting.

Salem killing every creature he can find. Becoming obsessed with extending his life so he can hunt forever. Killing a witch in Wick and then severing his bond with Max.

Catching Max spying on his meeting with Ashmedai in the forest and capturing Max.

Most of all, I see how much Max cared about Salem. How he tried and tried to pull him back from the path he'd started down, but in the end, there was nothing he could do. His friendship with Salem was slowly tearing him apart, turning him into someone he wasn't.

I know then that the same thing almost happened to me.

I never stopped to think that just because Salem is a Raven doesn't mean he's perfect. He was Max's friend, but he was also lost and didn't want to be found.

Max's friendship with Salem was bad for him, just like it was bad for me. He fueled my anger. Twisted my pain. He brought all the worst parts of me out instead of the good ones.

Toxic, I think, clinging to the word game that always grounds me. *Poisonous. Destructive.*

As the light fades, the bond settling into place, I look to Anna, the person who's only ever made me my best, who's gotten me through the worst of everything.

"I'm sorry," I tell her, feeling tears threaten. "I really messed up."

I wanted to believe in Salem so much. He said all the right things, all the ones I needed to hear. He wanted to make me a real Raven, said he believed in me, trusted me, and I couldn't see past that. I didn't want to.

"I kind of lost myself," I say.

Anna's smile wobbles. "I'm just glad you're back." She throws her arms around me, squishing Max between us. He makes a noise of protest.

A noise I *feel.*

Max? I think, and a sensation of distinct displeasure comes floating back to me. I squeeze Anna one more time, then let her go to find Max glowering up at us.

"I think I can . . . understand him?" I say cautiously.

Anna grins. "I wondered if you would. It seemed like he and Salem were communicating in the visions I saw."

Something akin to an eye roll comes down the bond, and Max leaps out of my hands, immediately beginning to sort his fur back into place as if he hadn't just almost died. Again!

Henry joins us—I hadn't even seen him wandering into the trees to give us space—and says, "I think I know what part of the woods we're in." He points behind him. "There's a lake down that way that's at the heart of the wood, which means town is a few miles west, and Ravenfall is a couple hours hike northward."

"How is that possible?" I ask, clambering to my feet and pulling Anna to hers.

"Space works differently in the two realms," he replies. "What was several days' worth of journeying there is only a few hours' worth here."

"That means we have time until Salem comes after us," Anna says with relief. "Since it'll take him a while to reach a portal."

"And time to rest," Henry adds with a pointed look at me. "Let's make camp here and head home around noon."

"No, we should keep moving," I say. "The sooner—"

I cut off as a wave of dizziness strikes me, and I sway. Anna grabs hold of my arm, steadying me, but my body feels like a sandbag.

"I think you used a lot of energy healing Max," she says, helping me to sit down before I collapse. Max climbs immediately into my lap, curls up, and goes to sleep mid-purr.

"But Salem—" I say groggily.

"Won't wake up for a while yet," Henry reassures me, already unrolling a sleeping bag.

I frown, thinking of how Salem collapsed. "What did you do to him?"

Henry grins, and it looks so much like Anna's, I do a double take. "Changed the word on the stone he used for the wards to 'sleep.'"

They catch me up on everything that happened on their end as they set up camp, Anna finishing with Max's arrival and revelation of Salem's history. I do the same, telling them how erratic Salem started acting and how I finally let myself access the powers I inherited from Fin.

The part about Salem calling me a monster I keep to myself. I don't want to talk about it yet.

"I think I was seeing his soul," I tell them. "Or his magic or life or something. I don't really know. But it looked really bad."

"Salem has been siphoning off powerful magical objects for a long time," Henry says as he hands out brisket sandwiches once we're gathered around the fire. "There's no telling what effect it's had on him and his body."

Anna's lips purse in thought. "I wonder if that's why he had you take the Myrtle Staff off the wall. Maybe he couldn't?"

"It would certainly explain why he was so nervous when you read the pedestal," Henry says thoughtfully. "I wouldn't be surprised if he was the one who broke it to begin with."

"That must be why he came to us for help in the first place," Anna adds. "He needed us to get the staff."

Henry winces. "I suppose he was just using me as a front. He wanted you kids to come all along—Colin to retrieve the staff and Anna to use it to find the tree—but he knew I wouldn't let you go alone."

I shiver with the memory of the power surging through Salem

when he accessed the tree's magic. "Whatever he's done to himself, it's made him really powerful. I could barely fight him."

Henry runs a frustrated hand through his curls. "I owe you kids an apology. Salem was my friend, and I failed to see who he was. I feel terrible for letting this happen, but I'm going to help you put it right."

Anna squeezes her dad's hand, and he wraps an arm around her.

Max lifts his head and blinks sleepily. A feeling of reassurance comes through the bond, followed by a burst of magic that nearly takes my breath away, chasing away the edges of my exhaustion. It takes me a second to realize what he means as the magic echoes through me.

"I can draw from your power now?" I ask, and he nods.

Tentatively, I reach out along our link. His magic is cool and flighty, but I can feel it waiting for me if I need it—and I will if I'm going to face Salem again.

Thanks, I think, and the feeling that comes back is warm, and a little sorry. I raise an eyebrow, and Max sends something more specific: an explanation. After everything that happened between him and Salem, he never thought he'd want to bond with another Raven, but he's happy it's me.

"Me too," I say, and realize it's not just Max that I'm glad to have on my side. I got so caught up in looking for Salem's approval that I forgot I already had a circle of people supporting me. Liam and I might disagree sometimes, and Anna and I may argue, but they've always been here for me, just like I will be for them.

We catch a couple hours of sleep before Henry wakes us around noon and we pack up camp, starting our walk back to Ravenfall. I feel a little bruised and stiff, but thanks to my Raven powers, the worst of it has already healed. Max is almost back to perfect form.

"That's strange," Henry says as the trees begin to thin a couple hours into traveling. "The house ought to be right, well, there."

He points to a series of tightly pressed oaks lined up like sentinels. They're half on top of each other, roots intertwining and branches practically interwoven as if to create a barrier. Weak streams of sunlight escape through the thin gaps, but thick bushels of bramble plug up most of them like bundled spiderwebs. After spending the last few weeks hunting in these woods with Elaine, Roy, and Liam, I know the area pretty well, and I've never seen anything like that near Ravenfall.

Anna approaches one of the trunks and says, "Excuse me? Can we get through please?"

The oak rustles, disgruntled, but it loosens its branches, leaning a little to the right to create an opening. We squeeze through one by one into what should have been the sloping grass field surrounding Ravenfall.

Except it's gone.

Trees have erupted from every square inch, creating a canopy thick enough to dampen the sun.

And in the center, Ravenfall has been consumed by the Hollowthorn Woods.

CHAPTER 20

Anna

"Aunt Elaine! Uncle Roy!" I shout as I rush up to what remains of the front stairs, which are covered in snow-dusted moss and roots. Colin, Henry, and Max follow, and we fight our way up to the deck, ducking under branches and slipping on frosted leaves.

The front door hangs off its hinges, and we pile into the foyer, where trees shoot out of the floor and continue past the high ceiling into the levels above. Leaves blanket the ground like a forest floor, branches twisting around railings and along doorways. The Christmas tree lies on its side, blocking the staircase, and roots have grown over it. A wisp bobs in and out of the branches, its light reflecting on a half-buried menorah.

It's like the house has been abandoned for centuries and reclaimed by nature—except we've only been gone for seven days.

"Elaine, Roy!" Henry calls, but no one answers. The house is as still as a forest at midwinter—it's even snowing from the ceiling, the flakes evaporating before they hit the floor. The air is damp and cold like after a hard rain.

Colin and I head for the kitchen, but when we push through the door, we step onto a sidewalk.

Willow Street in downtown Wick stretches before us, the witches' cottages on the left in brightly colored pastels, the Wicked Orchid flower shop on our right. Dilara—Rose's girlfriend—waves at us from the shop window before she realizes there's a door into a forest open behind us and her brow furrows.

"What the heck is happening?" Colin asks with that all-encompassing frown of his.

"I don't know." My voice trembles and I grab his arm, pulling him back through and closing the door.

Henry is down the hall, peering into the library. "This door leads to the Gemstone Forest in Sheol!"

The downstairs bathroom door goes to my bedroom and the door to Henry's study to the backyard, and through them all, we find no trace of Aunt Elaine or Uncle Roy. I ask the house for help, but it doesn't respond. I've never seen it so still.

"I'm sure they're okay," Colin says when I slam yet another door in frustration. "Elaine and Roy have dealt with stranger things than this."

"But what *is* this?" I gesture at the devastated house. It looks worse than it did after the fight with Fin. I barely recognize it, and seeing it so cold, so lifeless, makes my heart hurt.

Max comes bounding down the stairs, flicking his tail urgently back the way he came. We all struggle past the fallen Christmas tree and follow him upstairs, carefully picking our way up to the fourth floor and down the hall to Uncle Roy's room.

I stop on the other side of the threshold with a gasp. A massive branch wraps around Aunt Elaine and Uncle Roy like a ribbon. Their eyes are closed, and they hang limply in the tree's grasp.

"Aunt Elaine, Uncle Roy!" I call.

Aunt Elaine stirs first, followed by Uncle Roy, and my heart unclenches. "You're okay," I say as we move deeper into the room. "What happened?"

Uncle Roy groans and shifts in his bark prison. "We really don't know."

"The house started acting strangely a few days ago," Aunt Elaine says wearily. "Burning food, delivering baggage to the wrong place. Then creatures from the wood started showing up, and floors started disappearing, and before we knew it Hollow-thorn had engulfed the place—and us."

"Nora's gonna kill us," Uncle Roy says, then adds, "I really need to pee."

Henry inspects the branches. "Have you tried burning your way out?"

Uncle Roy snorts and wiggles the fingers on his left hand, which is immobilized by branches. "The trees didn't take kindly to it."

I walk to the nearest wall and lay my hand on a patch not covered by vines. The house's usual thrum of magic is gone, but there's something else there.

Taking a deep breath, I begin building a bridge of magic between me and the house I've lived in all my life. I pull memories into it: the house waking me each morning with a gentle rumble, the spiced scent of apple pie baking downstairs, the way it always stretches and settles in the sun, like a cat curling up for a nap.

The house welcomes me, reaching back, though faintly. I seize hold, and the story spills out of the house with ease.

I see it losing control of its magic, see the woods consuming it, taking its power. I feel the trees' fear, and I follow that fear to the source: a man who has come to destroy them.

"It was Salem," I say as I pull free of the reading. "Hollowthorn sensed he was up to something with the Tree of Life and came looking for help. It took the house's magic to reinforce itself when Salem started to drain the power of the tree."

"Wait," Uncle Roy says. "What?"

Colin catches them up on what happened in the Otherworld, from Salem tricking us into retrieving the Myrtle Staff for him to his manipulation of Colin and his past relationship with Max.

"He wants to use the staff to absorb the Tree of Life's power and become immortal," Colin finishes. "But if he does that, the Otherworld will die, and magic will too."

Uncle Roy sighs. "Here we go again."

"That must be why he felt so powerful to me." Elaine's eyes roll up in thought. "And why he wore that gold ring to prevent himself from being read."

Henry opens the bathroom door, peers out, and then closes

199

it with a frown. "Some of these link to Sheol. It's very possible that Salem will be able to find a place to cross over much sooner than we anticipated."

Colin peers out the nearest window at the encroaching wood. "Defeating him might be the only way to get the forest to retreat."

"And how exactly are we going to do that?" I ask. "He's the oldest, most powerful Raven ever."

Aunt Elaine blows a piece of hair out of her face. "You said that he's been absorbing magic from a bunch of different sources to extend his life, right?" Colin nods and she continues. "Well, we know someone who has the ability to manipulate life magic."

She looks pointedly at Colin, who winces.

"You don't have to use your powers if you don't want to," I tell him, but he shakes his head.

"No, I think I'm ready to." He says it hesitantly, but I see the resolve in his face. "He's lived too long already, and he has to be stopped. If I take his stolen life magic, his aging should catch up with him. But I don't want to absorb it like Fin."

"You can't just release that much powerful magic either," Uncle Roy says. "Who knows what will happen?"

Henry's face lights up. "Then we trap it. Anna, do you remember that chest you were experimenting with when I got home?"

I nod, thinking of the wooden chest with the hamsa carved on the side. I'd taken it back to Henry's study before we left for the Otherworld.

"It can hold magic, though I'm not exactly sure how it works," Henry says.

"Meaning I'll have to read it to find out," I say with a groan. Great. The one object I can't make speak a word to me is our only hope for preventing Salem's power from running rampant after Colin extracts it. Why can't our plans ever rest on something easy, like making tea?

"How do we get to Henry's study, though?" Colin surveys the room. "None of the doors go where they're supposed to."

"The house still knows where everything is." I walk back to the wall and lay my hand on it again. "I think it'll be able to tell me which way to go."

I close my eyes and focus on my bridge with the house. Sure enough, it sends me a memory of what changed, forming a map in my mind of where everything leads.

"We, uh, have to jump down the laundry chute," I say.

"That should be interesting," Henry muses. "I'll come with you."

"And I'll try to get Roy and Elaine free before Salem arrives." Colin rolls up his sleeves.

"During which we'll help you access your new powers," Aunt Elaine adds with far too much excitement.

Uncle Roy sighs. "I just really want to pee."

CHAPTER 21

Anna

Henry and I pick our way over roots and under branches toward the laundry chute down the hall. He's characteristically silent the entire way, and I feel like I should say something, but even after spending a week straight with him, I still don't know how.

I fiddle nervously with the Seal of Solomon in my pocket, which Colin gave me to lock in the study. He'd explained the magic had nearly been too much for him to use, and he didn't want to risk summoning Ashmedai again, which made hiding it from Salem the next best thing.

The laundry chute door is covered in vines, and I have to tear them away to open it. They shudder and shoot outward, taking over a nearby wall.

"Are you sure about this?" Henry peers over my shoulder at the cylindrical opening.

"Nope!" I try for a reassuring smile, but nothing feels okay right now. Seeing the house like this has really shaken me. I just want everything to go back to the way it was.

"Right." Henry takes a deep breath. "I'm going first, then."

I step aside as he hooks his legs over the ledge, mutters something in what sounds like Hebrew, and then pushes off. I hear a distant "Whoa!" and then silence.

"Henry?" I call down the chute.

A beat, and then, "I'm okay! Come down."

I shuffle onto the ledge and let go, barreling down the chute like a slide. It's not the first time I've flown down it—to the house's dismay—but I usually land in a soft heap of clothing in the laundry room. This time, I come flying out into the air as if someone threw me through the study door.

A strong pair of arms catches me, and I blink up at Henry's bewildered face. "That looked even stranger from this perspective," he says.

"Thank the ancient tree magic," I mutter, trying to get my heart out of my throat.

Henry sets me on my feet and surveys his study. It's been left entirely untouched by the trees' assault, except for a few items that fell off the crowded wood shelves in all the shaking.

"This room is heavily warded by magic other than the house's," Henry says to my confused look. "I had to make sure all the objects I brought back with me were safe."

I bite back a comment about having his priorities straight and cross the study to where the wooden chest rests. I set the Seal of

Solomon down beside it, then slide the chest off the shelf. It feels as cold and lifeless as ever in my hands, and my stomach starts to knot with anticipation.

What if I can't do this?

Salem's magic is ancient and powerful. If Colin pulls it out of him and just lets it go, it'll be like unleashing the energy of a bomb.

Ravenfall wouldn't survive. *We* might not survive.

"Anna?" Henry's voice is soft, and I turn to find him leaning back against his great oak desk. I've always loved that desk—it reminds me of him. Sturdy, austere, its dark wood the exact color of his hair and beard. When I see it, it means I'm in his study, listening to a story from his latest adventure.

It means he's home.

Henry rubs a hand along his jaw, looking uncomfortable. "I owe you an apology."

I blink, not expecting that at all. "For what?"

"For not being here for you as much as I should have," he replies. "Ravenfall . . . this place has always been difficult for me. I love you all very much but being the only one here without any sort of magic always made me feel like a fish out of water."

My chest pangs with a familiar feeling. I know exactly what Henry is talking about. It's how I felt a couple months ago, when I couldn't use my powers to help the inn while the rest of my family—and even Colin—did.

I felt useless, like I didn't belong here.

"Searching for magical objects became my way of connecting

with the magic in our lives," he continues. "But instead of using it to build a bridge between us, I used it as a place to hide. Because people . . . people are difficult for me."

I start to say that's an understatement but stop, realizing that might only make him uncomfortable. Maybe all I need to do is listen.

"I struggle with social anxiety, and it makes talking to people a challenge." A small smile tugs at his lips. "Your mother calls it my 'seven-second rule.' That's about how long I can last before it just gets too stressful. I've gotten better at it recently, but it's not something I've ever known how to talk about."

He lets out a heavy breath, looking up at me. "But I love you very much, Anna, and these last few days with you have been a light. I am so proud of you."

With every word, the image I have of my dad shifts a little, until the space that's always been between us shrinks away. This whole time I've been trying to decide who he is: explorer or scholar, father or stranger. Instead of listening, I made assumptions and stuck by them.

I did the same thing with Colin and Salem, standing my ground even when Colin got upset, and I'm proud of myself for that. But I realize now that I didn't listen to Colin either, only kept telling him what I thought, when both are possible.

Like a contradiction, I think, remembering Henry's explanation back in Sheol. *It forces you to really think and try to understand something.*

I can disagree and have my own opinion while still listening to Colin's, and just because we don't agree doesn't mean we can't get along.

I just have to listen, like I always want people to listen to me.

If I had, maybe then I'd have realized why Henry always looks uncomfortable when he's talking to someone, or why even though he's gone so often, he always brings me something back, because he's thinking of me even when he's not here. I'd have realized that all those funny sweaters, and the talk of magical objects and their stories, were his way of trying to connect.

"I felt that way about Ravenfall too," I tell him. "I didn't think I belonged here, and it took me a really long time to realize that Ravenfall didn't need me to be like everyone else: it just needed me to be me."

It was my powers that worked on Fin on Samhain, me who realized that he and his wraiths had tricked us into thinking Colin was dangerous, and it's me who's going to figure out this chest and trap Salem's magic where it can't hurt anyone.

Henry's nervous expression softens, and I say, "The inn needs all of us, and we all need each other."

He steps forward, enveloping me in a hug. I lean into him, peering up. "I'm really glad you're here."

"Me too," he says, offering a reassuring smile. It's as terrible as mine. "And when this is over, we can talk more about my side of the family if you want. I know I haven't been forthcoming about that either."

I pull back, clutching the chest close. "The way I feel about being Jewish is like the way you feel about Ravenfall. Full fish mode."

He laughs. "Well, then, maybe we have some things to learn from each other."

I grin back at him and hold up the wooden chest. "Starting with this."

CHAPTER 22

Colin

I pace along Roy's room, Max perched on my shoulder, and try to work up the courage to dip into Fin's magic again.

"It's just like your Raven powers," Elaine says encouragingly. Her face is half obscured by a branch at this angle, but I can't see her and Roy at the same time, which is why I started pacing. Now it's the only thing keeping my nervous energy under control.

"I know," I say. "I can feel it. I just . . ."

Fin's magic sits inside me like a burst of mist that slipped under my skin. It's been clamoring for my attention for weeks and I've been trying to keep it under control, but it's like the more I shove it down, the more it pushes back up. Since I used it on Salem, it's been practically screaming at me.

"Using that power doesn't make you like him, Colin," Roy says gently.

No, I nearly did that to myself. The last few weeks all I could think about was getting stronger, better, faster. I wanted more power, more strength, just like Fin. We both thought we were doing the right thing, that we were protecting the people we care about. If it weren't for Anna, I might have ended up just like him.

But using his magic feels different. It feels like opening a connection between us, one I'm not sure I want, especially when I still *feel so angry.*

"Fin's magic was a part of him," I say through gritted teeth. "If I use it . . ."

"I know a thing or two about having a complicated relationship with your abilities." Roy waves his fingers, where his pale skin is marked with burn scars. "It took a long time before I learned to keep my own fire from burning me, and longer still to stop hurting people around me with it."

"I would know," Elaine mutters darkly.

Roy flashes a grin she can't see and says, "But your magic is your magic. It's a part of you. And shutting parts of yourself away—it never works."

"He's right," Elaine says. "You keep calling these powers Fin's magic. But it isn't his, Colin. It's yours."

"Mine," I repeat quietly, staring down at my hands. On instinct, I summon my Saint Knives. Their cool touch steadies me as it always does, but I look at them differently. Because these are another thing that once belonged to Fin before they were mine, and I can't imagine myself without them now.

They're a part of me, just like these new powers, and trying to lock them away isn't the answer.

This is what Saoirse meant when she asked if I knew who I was. She could tell that I was smothering this part of myself. But if I want to use Fin's magic—*my* magic—to protect Ravenfall, I have to accept that it's a part of me too.

I let the blades return to my journal, and with them goes the tightness in my chest. Because it wasn't just the magic that I needed to accept—it was also the constantly burning flame of anger in my gut. Anger at my parents for lying to me for so long, then not being there to tell me the truth. Anger at Liam for treating me like a child, instead of the Raven I wanted to be.

Anger at myself for not being able to talk to anyone about it, because it makes me feel vulnerable, and that scares me.

And I'm so tired of being afraid.

I don't want to become a monster like Fin. I want to be strong enough to protect the people I care about, so I don't lose someone else.

But I can't let my fear control me. It's okay to be angry, and it's okay to be scared.

"I can do this," I say, and dive into the magic.

It welcomes me like a long-lost friend. Like before, my vision shifts, everything taking on a blue tinge. I see the burn of Elaine's and Roy's souls, the bright gold laced with the silver of their magic.

Max glows like a wisp on my shoulder, and the branches and roots light up like Christmas trees, setting the whole room afire.

"Wow," I breathe.

Then something happens.

The roots and branches of the trees begin to writhe and twist, as if in warning. The whole house shudders and groans.

In the hallway, a door clicks open.

CHAPTER 23

Anna

The house shakes, and I throw a hand against the wall, reaching for my magic and diving into its memories. An image of the fourth floor materializes, and I watch as a door opens and Salem steps through.

"He's here." A chill tickles the back of my neck, and I peer down at the lifeless box in my hands. Hopefully Colin will be okay distracting Salem while I figure out how to use it.

"Can you tell me about the chest?" I ask Henry. "I . . . still can't read it."

He hesitates before saying, "I told you before that it was gifted to me by a Jewish witch, but what I didn't say is that witch is my sister."

I blink—my aunt is a *witch*? I only met her once briefly when she came to visit Ravenfall years ago, but I never saw her do any magic.

"Bubbe," I say, thinking of the vision in which she brought Max to Ravenfall after Salem killed her sister. "She's one, too, and your sister inherited it, and you . . ."

"Didn't," Henry says with a smile. "It's always run through the maternal line of our family. I was jealous as a kid, so my sister was always finding and spelling magical objects for me. She gave this box to me not long after our father died to, quote, 'hold all of my precious magical objects.' She meant it facetiously, of course."

"Fleshy what?"

"Facetiously. It means 'sarcastically.'"

I file that one away to use on Colin.

"She's another person that I owe an apology to," he says with a sigh. "I think I've known that for a long time, and maybe that's why I never actually put anything in the chest. It's been sitting on that shelf for years."

Something about what he says sticks with me. The chest has a lonely air to it, like I can feel its solitude. It learned to sit alone on its shelf, unbothered by everything else around it, and now that I'm here trying to pry my way into it, it wants nothing to do with me.

I take the details Henry gave me and gather my magic, forming a bridge. But even as I reach out, the chest's story in my mind, I know that it's useless.

I can't make this object speak.

Henry must see me struggling to read it, because he joins me by his desk where I've set the chest. It only makes me more nervous having him right there, watching me mess up.

"Is it not speaking to you?" he asks, and I shake my head. If I can't get the chest to tell me how it works, we won't be able to trap Salem's magic when Colin removes it, and who knows what will happen?

I set my hand on its lid and try again, but there's nothing.

"Do you need me to tell you more about it?" he asks, and my nerves twist tighter. This is supposed to be our thing. He tells me about the objects, and then I use their stories to connect to them. Thanks to this expedition, I've talked more with my dad than ever before.

If we don't have this to bond over, what will we talk about? Will he feel uncomfortable and leave again when this mess is over?

I look up at Henry, at the concern so obvious in his face, but also the glimmer of something else. Something like curiosity. He wants to tell me more about the chest, just like he always wants to tell me about magical objects. Because that's what he loves to do, just like I love being at Ravenfall and helping guests.

This is his way of connecting, and everyone's way is different. Maybe the same is true of magical objects. This whole time I've been trying to force the chest to tell me its story, and for some objects that works, but for this one, I think I need to try something else.

"Sure," I say. "Whatever you can think of."

Henry scratches his beard in thought. "Well, there's the time I found Max asleep in it," he says, and starts off on the story.

As he talks, I focus on the chest, but instead of trying to build a bridge of magic to it, I just . . . listen.

Something stirs inside it, a feeling of familiarity, as if it knows this story. It remembers Max flipping open its lid with his nose and climbing inside. Remembers how warm it got, and the fur he left behind. Bit by bit the story stretches out to me, interlacing with my magic, and the bridge between us takes hold.

I ask it how to use its magic, and it sends me a memory of a woman who looks a lot like Henry: dark hair, thick brows, brown eyes that have shades of gold in the sunlight. She says something in Hebrew over the chest, and the hamsa on the front glows bright.

I pull free of the memory, and something settles into place inside me, like a missing piece. With how distant Henry is from his family, I've only met my aunt once, and I was young enough that I barely remember her. Seeing her again, feeling her magic—it feels like getting to know my dad a little better. Like there's a whole slew of stories there, waiting to be told.

Once this is over, I want to hear every single one.

I do my best to repeat the words back to Henry, but I only remember a few of them, and I stumble over the Hebrew.

A smile pulls at his lips. "I know it. It's a blessing for the home, often inscribed on hamsas."

He takes a piece of paper and writes out the blessing. Then he reads it aloud to me, and I repeat it back to him best I can, my tongue twisting on the unfamiliar words. I wish I knew what they meant, but it's just another thing I'll have to ask Henry about when this is all over.

"We just have to say that while holding the chest, and it will seal Salem's magic inside," I explain, grabbing the chest off the desk. "Now let's go find Colin."

CHAPTER 24

Colin

Max leaps down from my shoulder, and we step into the hallway, where Salem stands. The door he came through clicks shut behind him, and for a moment, it's like we're back in the Otherworld, him leading me into the trees to start training.

But there's something different about him now—a look in his eyes that turns me cold.

"I see even that infernal wood has decided to interfere," Salem says. His clothes are torn and muddy, his hair wild as if he rushed all the way here. The Otherworld doesn't seem like a kind place to a human alone, and I wonder what he faced to get here.

"Please don't do this, Salem," I say. "You don't have to take the tree's power. You can still protect people without it."

"For how long? A few more years before my body begins to break down?" Salem shakes his head. "There are so few of us left now. The tide is shifting in the enemy's favor, and I won't let it."

He's not wrong. The population of Ravens has been dwindling naturally across the centuries, and after Fin and his wraiths made it their goal to hunt us down to weaken the Shield, there's even fewer left. How many monsters hurt people every day because Ravens aren't there to protect them?

Salem holds out a hand to me. "Come with me, Colin. I can share this power with you, and together, we can make a real difference. We can protect everyone, and make sure what happened to you never happens to anyone else again."

I want so badly to believe him.

If someone as powerful as him had been around when my family needed him, maybe my parents would still be alive. Maybe they would be teaching me to be a Raven right now. How many others are there with a story like mine? Like his? How many will there be without him?

But I can't ignore the things Salem has done. Max showed me the dark path he took, and I saw for myself the impact it had on Salem's soul. He wants to eradicate every supernatural being, to take magic from the world and keep it for himself.

Maybe, once, he was trying to do the right thing, but not anymore.

"Come with me," he says again. "We can be a family."

At that, I shake my head, thinking of Liam and Anna and Max and everyone else at Ravenfall. "I already have a family."

Bit by bit, Salem's affable expression falls away, until he's all but snarling at me. "Your family abandoned you."

"What?" I step back.

"They hid your Raven powers from you for years," he says. "Your parents died because they were too proud, just like you."

A terrible, creeping feeling settles in my gut. "What are you saying?"

Salem sneers. "I once offered your mother the same thing I'm offering you, but she refused me. I tried again when Fin was hunting you down, and still, she wouldn't listen."

He stares me straight in the eye as he says, "So I told Fin where to find them in exchange for a boost from his life magic."

It takes a moment for his words to sink in. *He's* the reason Fin found my parents. *He's* the reason that they're gone.

I expect to be angry, to want to scream at him or lash out, but I just feel empty.

Max, on the other hand, lets out a Jabberwocky-sized roar and transforms, leaping at Salem.

Salem throws himself into the wall, and Max lands, turning on him, but Salem's already got his knives in hand. He slashes at Max's shoulder, opening a silver wound. Max growls and just barely grazes Salem across the arm with his claws as Salem flees down the hall.

He seizes the nearest door and thrusts it open, stepping through.

I summon my Saint Knives and go after him.

The hallway door opens into the Faerie Gardens in downtown Wick. Many of the trees have lost their leaves, the trunks painted with thick coats of moss, and the evening's mist is already setting in.

Salem is waiting for me beneath an oak. I go straight for him, already diving into my life magic. He deflects my strikes, but I'm half focused on the roiling mass of energy in his chest.

I try reaching for it, but my powers don't respond. I must have to be touching him to extract it, the same way I was in the Otherworld.

Salem lunges, his knife catching along my arm, and I stumble. Then Max is there, driving Salem back. Salem's knives vanish, and the quarterstaff he used against the Shamir Worm appears in his hands.

"Give me the Myrtle Staff and I won't hurt you," he says, but I'm done listening to his lies. I lunge for him, and he ducks around me, swinging the quarterstaff at Max's flank. It hits hard, sending him tumbling.

"Max!" I move toward him, but he's already back up, his tail lashing angrily.

I step between them. "Wait, Max. All he wants is the staff."

Which means we don't even have to fight him—we just have to delay him until Anna and Henry are ready for me to extract his magic. Then we'll attack.

Catching my meaning, Max shrinks into a cat and darts back through the door to Ravenfall. I follow, Salem snarling in frustration.

Except the door doesn't go to the hallway anymore.

Instead, it dumps us out in an unfamiliar shop, the walls full of hooks displaying various types of hats, from sea-blue sun hats to stiff top hats. Salem tumbles in after us, startling a pair of older shoppers that I recognize as Mr. and Mrs. Andrade from the animal shelter down the road.

"Colin?" Mrs. Andrade asks in surprise.

"Hi!" I duck under Salem's fist, then drive my foot into his stomach. "Sorry!"

Mr. Andrade looks between us, then seizes a baseball cap from the nearest rack and brings it down atop Salem's head. The moment it strikes, Salem's hands jerk up over his shoulder and he drops into a batting stance, ready to swing at an imaginary ball.

I remember Anna's warning months ago to never put on the house's hats, and now I see why—they're all enchanted.

"Thanks!" I call to the Andrades before tackling Salem back through the portal. The last thing I want is for our fight to spill across Wick.

We tumble across the floor of the ballroom at the back of Ravenfall. Normally full of twinkling lights and mist twisting into various shapes, it's completely overgrown by the wood. The roots lash at us, and we both spin away, the baseball hat having come free of Salem's head.

"The portals are changing," I say to Max. "I think the magic is getting more unstable."

Salem surges back to his feet, but Max and I are already running. We head for the nearest door, but instead of ending up on the back deck, we appear in Ravenfall's rooftop garden—right in the middle of the ice-skating rink.

"Whoa!" I throw out my hands for balance, skidding across the ice. Max goes flat as a pancake, all four paws splaying in different directions.

Salem flies through the door after us, and we scramble to move across the ice. The ground shakes as Salem brings his quarterstaff down into it, ice cracking down to the foundation. He uses it as leverage to hurry across the ice faster than we can move.

When he's only a few feet away, Max transforms, swinging his tail around and catching Salem in the chest. He goes skidding across the ice, and we scramble the last few feet to the rink door, leaping through.

We appear in Hollowthorn Woods, right beside the massive oak tree, Grandpa. The other oaks rustle their leaves and sway side to side, their fear nearly as strong as my growing panic.

Because we're out of doors to jump through.

"Enough." Salem emerges behind us and slams the door shut. Blood trickles down the side of his head, but he still clutches his quarterstaff.

Max and I face him, my Saint Knives back in my hands. Salem strikes with the quarterstaff, and I dance aside. Before Salem can pull back, Max's jaws lock around the quarterstaff. He wrenches it out of Salem's hands and snaps it in two with one powerful bite. Not missing a beat, knives appear in Salem's hands, and he slashes Max's muzzle.

Howling, Max drops back, and I try to disarm Salem, but he's so much faster than me. His knife catches my other arm, and then the front of my thigh. Then his knives disappear, and he comes at me with his bare hands before I've recovered from his other attack. He seizes my wrists, so much stronger than me, and drives his knee into my stomach.

I gasp, dropping my knives, but he holds me up. "The Myrtle Staff!" he commands. "Or when I'm finished with you, I will make sure Anna and Henry suffer the same fate."

"You're not a Raven anymore," I say, breathless. "You're a monster."

"What do you know?" Salem hisses. "You're just a child."

I flash him my best imitation of Anna's reckless grin. "I'm the descendant of the King of the Dead."

And then I *pull* on his magic as hard as I can.

Salem tries to draw away, but I seize his wrists. Then Max is there, his tail wrapping around Salem's body to hold him still. Fin's magic—*my* magic—courses through me, and I sense the presence of nearby spirits, of the wood's power, of the magic Wick is steeped in.

I feel Max reach out to me, and I let his power in. It strengthens me, letting me hold on as Salem thrashes, our strength equal.

"What are you doing to me?" he demands.

I pull harder. "I'm taking back all that life magic you stole!"

His magic starts to come free, hot and sharp and biting like lightning in my hands. It hurts, but I don't let go. It courses over my skin, crackling black and red. I hold it to me, afraid of what might happen if I let it disperse.

But I can't hold it forever. I can't hold Salem forever.

I need Anna.

CHAPTER 25

Anna

Henry and I fly through the house, following the path of doors the house gave me. Through a bedroom in the fourth-floor hallway and into the kitchen. Out the back door up to the ice rink in the garden, through the door, and—

"Colin!" I shout as we emerge in the clearing alongside Grandpa. "I have the chest!"

He and Max are holding Salem in place with raw strength, and Salem's magic is visible as it crawls up Colin's skin, crackling and red.

"Don't . . . do this," Salem grunts through gritted teeth. "You're making a mistake."

Colin hesitates—and it's all Salem needs.

He slams his forehead into Colin's, knocking him back, and then summons a blade that he drives into Max's tail. Max howls, releasing him.

Salem's magic retreats inside him, and he summons back his blade from Max, eyes locking on the chest in my hands. Before Colin or Max can recover, he charges at me. Henry jumps between us, and Salem brings his knife down.

"No!" I scream.

The knife rebounds backward as if striking a force field, throwing Salem off his feet. On the chest's face, the hamsa glows a bright silver.

"It protected us," I whisper wonderingly.

Henry's face reflects my surprise, before melding into a fervent curiosity. "Fascinating," he murmurs.

Salem climbs gingerly back to his feet, staring at the symbol with wide eyes. "Hamsas protect from evil," he says. "I'm not . . . I can't be . . ."

Max's tail wraps around him, trapping his arms to his sides. Then Colin is there, his hand on Salem's shoulder as he tries to draw out his life magic again. The crackling energy reappears, creeping up Colin's arms.

"No!" Salem thrashes, but the hamsa's strike must have weakened him, and Max holds on.

"I can't pull it free," Colin grunts.

There must be some way to help him, except I don't have that kind of power.

But I know something that does.

I hand the chest to Henry. "Be ready to do the spell."

"Me?" he says, still pale from Salem's attack. "I don't have any powers."

"You don't need them," I say with a grin. "The magic's in the object."

I rush to Colin's side. "Can you summon the Myrtle Staff?"

He glances at me, looking a little dazed from Salem's earlier strike, but he doesn't argue. The staff appears in his other hand, and I take it.

With his target in reach, Salem struggles harder. I press the tip of the staff against his other shoulder and dive into its magic.

Colin said that Salem wants the staff to conduct the tree's power, and that means it can channel life magic.

Sure enough, I feel Salem's power on the other side of the staff. Then I pull.

Salem's magic gathers at the point of contact in a bright, sizzling light like the end of a sparkler, resisting my draw. Recognizing my plan, Colin grabs hold of the staff, too, ready to absorb the magic when it comes free. I pull harder, and Salem's power zips along the staff and rushes into Colin's hand. He grimaces at the sudden influx but bears it. The magic bites at our skin and singes our fingers, but we both draw it out as hard as we can.

"Henry!" I yell, but he's already there.

Colin seizes the roiling mass of crackling red and black magic and thrusts it into the chest. Henry slams the lid closed and recites the blessing in Hebrew. The hamsa comes alight once more, sealing the chest shut.

Salem cries out as his body begins to change. His skin wrinkles and withers, his eyes sinking inward and his fingers curling up.

Max releases him, and Salem collapses to his knees, staring in horror at his changing body. Without the magic extending his life, his age is catching up to him, and quickly.

He moans, reaching for the staff with the last of his strength.

A root loops around his ankle. Then another around his wrist, his waist, his chest.

Grandpa unravels, revealing the portal into Sheol, and the Hollowthorn Woods drags Salem through.

CHAPTER 26

Anna

The rest of the wood retreats with the disappearance of Salem.

The trees dive back into the earth, the roots coiling backward like reeled ropes, until the clearing between the wood and the house is nothing but grass. I shiver at the sudden silence, Salem's cries still echoing in my head. For a moment all I can do is breathe and try not to feel like a rag someone wrung dry.

It's over, but just like with Fin, I know it isn't really. We didn't walk away from that battle unchanged, and we won't walk away untouched from this one either. But we'll figure it out together, just like we did before.

I look to Colin, who stares forlornly into the woods. "Are you okay?"

"I don't know," he says. He's clutching his injured arm to his chest and leaning into Max for support.

Henry lays a hand on his shoulder, the chest tucked under his other arm. "That's okay too."

Colin squeezes his eyes shut as if fighting back tears, but when he opens them again, they're dry. "I wish we could have helped him."

"Salem made his choices," Henry replies. "He's responsible for them."

I wonder what will happen to him in the Otherworld, if he's even there. The wood's magic is incredibly powerful, beyond even our understanding. He might not have survived long enough to be dragged through, his body breaking down under the accumulated centuries.

Max shrinks back to his cat form, and Colin scoops him up. Both of them look worse for wear, covered in scrapes and cuts that have already started to heal thanks to the magic in their veins. Still, they could both do with a visit from the first aid kit.

I heft the staff over my shoulder. "Let's go inside and get you two patched up."

We climb the steps to the deck and follow it around to the kitchen side door. The inside is a mess, with holiday decorations strewn everywhere and holes in the walls and floor from where the roots and trees burst through. There are enough leaves on the ground to fill a swimming pool.

"Anna!" Aunt Elaine is helping Uncle Roy through the hall door. They both look pale, their skin scraped and bruised, but otherwise okay.

"You're free!" I rush over to help her with Uncle Roy, and they both sit down at the kitchen table.

Henry sets the chest on the counter, and Colin slides onto one of the stools. Max remains curled up in his arms, licking one of his own wounds.

"What happened with Salem?" Uncle Roy asks.

We recount everything for them, their eyes widening as we reach each new part of the story. We keep it short, none of us having much energy left to tell a longer tale.

"Then the wood took him," I finish with a shiver. I've always thought of the Hollowthorn trees as benevolent and kind, but I saw a darker side of them today that I never want to see again.

Uncle Roy shakes his head sadly. "What a shame."

Aunt Elaine looks to the wooden chest. "What will you do with it?"

"I thought I might return the staff to Sheol and leave the chest with it." Henry scratches his beard thoughtfully. "But then I worried they might not be safe there. After all, we found them and led a demon straight in."

"There aren't many places safer than Ravenfall," I say, even as I take in the damage to the house with a sinking feeling. "Or at least, there didn't used to be. Do you think the house is okay?"

When the house doesn't immediately rumble back at me, my heart sinks further.

"It probably just needs some time to recover," Aunt Elaine says gently.

Uncle Roy snorts. "We all do."

"I think I can help with that," says a voice from the doorway.

We all turn to find Rose gliding into the kitchen, her suitcase in one hand, bandages and salves in the other.

Kara follows, looking up from her phone long enough to say, "You are all so dead."

"We didn't do it!" I say at the exact same moment I hear Nora scream. "Roy Michael Ballinkay!"

Roy slumps in his seat with a groan. "Why is it always me?"

CHAPTER 27

Colin

Rose and Gran tend to everyone's wounds while Henry does his best to explain to a very red-faced Nora what happened while they were gone.

Liam, who gave everyone a ride back from the airport, leans in the kitchen doorway with his arms folded, listening without expression. When Henry reaches the part about Salem offering to train me, I want to slide under the table at the look of hurt on Liam's face. It only deepens when Henry reveals Salem's role in our parents' deaths.

Anna nudges my shoulder with hers while Rose applies a salve to the cuts on her hands. "Are you going to talk to him?"

"Yeah," I say with a sigh. "I wish he could just read minds like Kara; then I wouldn't have to say any of it."

"That's not how it works," Kara says from the stool beside him. "Not for the important stuff."

Rose puts a Band-Aid over the largest cut on Anna's hand. "Nothing is quite the same as talking." She's speaking to me, but it's Kara she gives a meaningful look to.

"What?" Kara demands, deliberately stubborn. She could just read Rose's mind if she wanted to know.

"Ask Anna," Rose says.

Anna sighs. "Ask Henry. He's not who you think he is, Kara. He loves us."

Kara's face flushes, and she goes back to whatever she was looking at on her phone with a grumble.

Henry finishes his story of what happened, and Liam locks eyes with me across the kitchen, heading my way. I gulp.

"Go on," Rose says. "He's just as nervous as you are."

For some reason hearing that makes me feel more confident. I slide off my stool and meet Liam halfway.

"Can we talk?" I ask.

He gives me a relieved smile. "Sure."

We head out onto the deck. Aside from a blanket of leaves and some gouges left by the roots, it's in pretty good shape considering what it went through. The late afternoon sun is low on the horizon, so that even though the air is chilly, the wood is warm when I lean on the railing, my boot crunching on some fallen thistle.

"I wish I'd been there with you," Liam begins. "In the Otherworld."

My anger spikes immediately. Already he's hinting that I couldn't handle what happened, that I would have needed his help. But I swallow back the urge to say that to him and instead ask, "Why?"

He blinks at me in surprise, as if he would have thought it obvious. "To keep you safe."

"Because you don't think I can do it myself?" I ask tightly.

"No, I— Is that what you've thought this entire time?" He pushes off the railing to face me, dew clinging to the arms of his leather jacket. I don't look at him, and it's enough of an answer for him to say, "I know how capable you are, Colin. The things you've done already as a Raven are incredible."

My hands curl around the railing. "Then why are you always trying to hold me back?"

"Because I'm terrified of losing you."

I look at him then, at the open fear and concern in his eyes. My resolve weakens. "But I can handle myself."

"I know that." He runs a nervous hand through his hair, sending it out in all directions. "It has nothing to do with how good you are. Mom and Dad were some of the best and look what happened to them."

I wince, but he's right. Even Salem, the most powerful Raven I've ever met, was defeated in the end.

"Mom and Dad weren't perfect, Colin," he says. "They made mistakes, and maybe keeping you from becoming a Raven was one of them, but they were only trying to keep you safe, like I am. What we do is dangerous. Even when you're good at it, things can go wrong. People get hurt. And I just . . . I wanted you to understand that before throwing yourself headfirst into it."

He attempts a smile, but it only looks sad. "I know how much being a Raven means to you. I'm sorry if I ever made you feel like you weren't good enough."

I roll onto my side against the railing to face him. "You're right, though. I do rush into things."

I give Anna such a hard time about speaking without thinking, but sometimes I do the same with my actions. I dove headfirst into the Otherworld and didn't stop until I'd almost helped a corrupt Raven destroy it without realizing it.

Things could have ended very differently today.

Liam loops an arm around my shoulders, pulling me into a hug that washes away the last of my tension. "We can both be a little right, and we can both be a little wrong," he says. "Sometimes that's just the way things are."

I lean into him, thinking of how our dad used to pull us both into one big hug. Mom, not wanting to be left out, would throw her arms around his neck from behind. Now my head nearly hits the bottom of Liam's chin, and it seems impossible that we could have once both fit inside Dad's arms. Maybe my parents weren't always perfect, but in moments like that, they were.

"I miss them," I say quietly.

Liam's arms tighten. "Me too."

CHAPTER 28

Anna

Nora shows no mercy.

After a good night's sleep, everyone is put to work the next morning restoring what we can of the house. We sweep leaves and twigs outside into piles and then into bags. We clean up broken decorations and set those still intact back in their proper places. The Christmas tree is righted, the menorah replaced in the kitchen window. By the time the sun begins to set, the house is sparking clean—and eerily silent.

I can't remember the last time we didn't have even a single guest. That would be strange enough, but the house still hasn't made a sound, and I'm starting to worry that it never will.

What if Hollowthorn took away all of its magic?

Max even went to the chimney to replace the house's fallen hat—a kippah for the last night of Hanukkah—and the house didn't acknowledge him.

Without the house's help, we all pitch in to cook dinner. The scent of brisket baking in the oven melds with buttery challah and frying latkes. Kara is holding a one-sided argument with Rose over whether sour cream or applesauce is better with them, while Rose prepares rugelach for dessert, lining the pastry dough with thick globs of chocolate ganache according to "how chocolatey the rugelach is feeling today."

Gran and Nora tell us about their trip to Ireland, which they spent mostly on the west side in Galway, traveling along the coast.

"It'll be the last vacation I ever take," Nora says, giving the entire kitchen a meaningful look.

"For the last time," Uncle Roy says with a groan. "This isn't my fault!"

"Anna *did* try to tell you something was wrong with the house, and you didn't listen," Aunt Elaine says, clearly trying to stoke the flames.

"Speaking of listening," Nora begins, her hands propped on her hips. "We're going to have a nice long conversation about making responsible choices. Like, I don't know, *not* sending children on a life-or-death mission into the Otherworld without at least giving me a call?"

Henry looks up from where he's rummaging through a drawer. "Well, technically, it was meant to be purely preventative and mostly educational, since—" He cuts off when he realizes Nora is one second away from hitting him with her spatula and changes course. "Um, yes. I'm free all evening."

Uncle Roy's laugh booms through the kitchen, and he and

Aunt Elaine descend into a bout of light-hearted teasing, but my heart feels anything but light. The food, the conversation—it all feels like it's missing something, and I know exactly what it is.

I press my hand to the nearest wall and whisper, "Can you hear me?" But the house is silent and cold. When I dive into the magic, its memories are there, but they're like any other object's.

My hand falls away, and I swallow hard against the tightness in my throat.

Henry emerges from his drawer search with a bundle of candles in hand and a lighter. He beckons me over to where the menorah now stands in the window. Made of blue and white porcelain, it's simple but elegant, and I try to focus on it instead of the house.

Henry sets a candle in each of the eight holders and points to the one in the center. "This candle is called the *shamash*. You use it to light all the others."

This isn't the first year that we've celebrated Hanukkah, but usually Henry handles it all himself, rushing through everything so that it's over before I even realize what he's done. Now that he's teaching me about it, I listen raptly, each word he speaks working away at the tightness in my chest. It's just the first on a list of a hundred questions I have about his side of our family, and I can't wait to learn more.

"Once we light it, I'll recite the Hanukkah blessings," he explains. "Then we'll use it to light the other candles from left to right."

He hands me the lighter as the rest of the family gathers

around us. Liam slings an arm over Colin's shoulders where he stands beside me, Max on his shoulder, and the twins behind us. Nora takes Henry's arm, while Uncle Roy helps Gran over, and Aunt Elaine sets her chin on his shoulder.

I remove the shamash and click the lighter, but it doesn't spark. Frowning, I shake it and try a couple more times, but nothing happens.

In the silence, the winter winds outside howl, and the house groans.

My heart leaps. Was it just the wind?

Then the candle's wick flickers—and comes alight.

Epilogue

The house is quiet, but it is a good kind of quiet.

The guests have all gone, and only the family remains. They've fixed the last of the damage—even the leak is finally gone—and everything has settled back into its rightful place.

The young Raven is out in the back field practicing with his older brother. Liam is in good spirits after his last phone call, and the house wonders when he will tell his brother about the person on the end who makes him smile.

The others sit around the bonfire, the flames sending shadows scurrying across the house's face.

A pyromaniac and a bookworm bicker over the best way to test Colin's new abilities. Roy makes the fire dance with a wave of his hand, and Elaine gestures to the book splayed open in her lap. The house wishes she wouldn't rely so heavily on the pressed remnants of trees past.

Some things cannot be found in books, and the house has had enough of trees.

Henry and Nora each clutch a tall glass of mulled wine the house prepared that morning, steeped with cinnamon and clove, and they hold hands and exchange bets as Kara and Rose play cards. Kara keeps showing her cards to Henry, asking for advice she doesn't need, and he gives it gladly.

It's the dulcet tones of Anna's voice the house seeks, though.

Her laughter settles into its eaves and runs along its dormers, a reminder that they are all safe, that they're home.

She's speaking to Henry's sister on the phone, an aunt the house has only met once. It liked her. She kept her room clean, and she made Anna laugh, as she does now. The house hopes they will see her again soon. Perhaps for the next holiday.

Yule is still a few days away, and whispers of the upcoming Wild Hunt play through Hollowthorn's leaves, when the fae will ride rampant through the trees in celebration of the changing season. Though the wood has retreated, the house feels it more than ever now. It left pieces of its power behind in the house's walls and in its floorboards, remnants that warm the house like the last coals of a smoldering fire.

Next time danger comes for its family, the house will be prepared.

But for now, it focuses on the little things. The challah loaf baking in its oven alongside a batch of snickerdoodles, the mugs of peppermint hot chocolate it's preparing for the family. It seeps into the faerie lights along the deck, making them twinkle and dance, and it breathes in a bundle of new mist, twirling it into shape after shape.

The mist spirals through the house and down through the library, where it rises up, up through the chimney, and brushes a cool breeze across the cat sleeping there.

Tonight, the house wears no hat.

Tonight, it is just the cat, and that is enough.

ANNA AND COLIN'S MAGICAL ADVENTURES
CONTINUE IN BOOK THREE
OF THE RAVENFALL SERIES....

WITCHWOOD

Coming Fall 2024!

ACKNOWLEDGMENTS

One of the things I like about writing acknowledgments is how it lets me look back at the journey of a story. When we sold this book, I had absolutely no idea what it was going to be about. All I knew is that it would be a direct sequel to *Ravenfall* that centered on Jewish mythology, and that I couldn't wait to start researching. During that process, I learned about so many cool things right alongside Colin and Anna, and I hope following their story has taught you something new too.

As always, my love to my Guillotine Queens for your constant support: Jessica Jones, Brittney Arena, Koren Enright, Jennifer Gruenke, Tracy Badua, Alyssa Colman, Ashley Northup, Rae Castor, and Sam Farkas. The best piece of advice I can give any new writer is to find a group of fellow writers to go through your journey with you; they're indispensable.

I can't believe I'm writing acknowledgments on book number four with my incredible agent, Carrie Pestritto. As always, thank you for handling my flood of emails and questions, and for always being there to help, talk about The Expanse, or make an impromptu cover mockup.

To my editor, Hannah Hill, for making me write my first-ever outline. I've never drafted a book so quickly and cleanly, and I may officially have been converted to an outliner (maybe . . . we'll see). You understand the heart of my stories on a level I didn't know was possible, and working with you has truly been an honor.

To my SprintitySprintSprints (I'm not letting this name go), Shannon and Joss—I would not have made it through this without our coffee dates. I'm so thankful to call you both friends, and to have the privilege of reading your amazing stories. Or at the very least, of yelling at you to write them. Love you both.

I'm endlessly grateful to my critique partners and friends Rosiee Thor, Linsey Miller, and Alexandra Overy for your open DMs and your support, and to Emily Lloyd-Jones for your hype help with book one. Manifesting good things for all of you!

Thank you so much to my fellow writers of Ash and Sheyd for your fact checking, pronunciation help, and rabbit hole conversations about Jewish lore. I'm so grateful for this community!

The entire Delacorte team has been a dream—thank you in particular to my publicist, Josh Redlich, for his enthusiasm and hard work, to Ken Crossland for the gorgeous interior designs, to Ramona Kaulitzki and Suzanne Lee for two incredible covers, and to everyone who helped make this book possible.

As always, thank you to my family and friends, to my mom and dad, and to the two little cats that keep me trapped at my writing desk.

Onward to book number five.

ABOUT THE AUTHOR

Kalyn Josephson is a fantasy author living in the California Bay Area. She loves books, cats, books with cats, and making up other worlds to live in for a while. She is the author of the Storm Crow duology and *Ravenfall*.

kalynjosephson.com